CW00524704

SLEEP EASY, BROTHER

Michael Cartwright

Sleep Easy, Brother

Michael Cartwright

Copyright © Michael Cartwright 2021

All rights reserved. No part of this publication may be reproduced, stored in a retrieval system or transmitted in any form or by any means electronic, mechanical, audio, visual or otherwise, without prior permission of the copyright owner. Nor can it be circulated in any form of binding or cover other than that in which it is published and without similar conditions including this condition being imposed on the subsequent purchaser.

Published by M D Cartwright Publishing in conjunction with Writersworld, this book is produced entirely in the UK, is available to order from most bookshops in the United Kingdom, and is globally available via UK-based Internet book retailers.

ISBN: 978-1-7398309-1-5

Cover design: Jag Lall

Copy editor: Sue Croft

WRITERSWORLD
2 Bear Close, Woodstock,
Oxfordshire
OX20 1JX
United Kingdom
www.writersworld.co.uk
Tel 01993 312500

The text pages of this book are produced via an independent certification process that ensures the trees from which the paper is produced comes from well managed sources that exclude the risk of using illegally logged timber while leaving options to use post-consumer recycled paper as well.

Dedication

To my wife Anna, for her support and patience

to my daughters Rachael and Victoria
and my son Dominick

I would also like to say thank you to Brian Skinner
for his help and encouragement.

*

Michael's first book, *The Yeoman's Challenge*,
is published by amazon.co.uk.
ISBN: 979-8-5588133-8-8

1

B en looked up at his big brother with admiration and a certain amount of jealousy.

'Where are you off to tonight? Are you clubbing it again?'

Jack turned from the mirror in their shared bedroom. 'I think I might just pay a visit to a club or two just to show my face.'

Enviously watching his brother get ready to go out on a Friday night had become a bit of a routine, but alas, Ben's age kept him from following. If only he could age five or six years in a day! As it was, it would be 1969 or even 1970 before they could go clubbing together.

'How old do you have to be to get into a club?' Ben asked with a certain amount of pleading in his voice.

'You've got at least another five years to go before I can take you with me.' Jack had a broad smile on his face as he ruffled his young brother's shock of fair hair. 'It'll come round sooner than you can imagine.'

Ben said grumpily that he couldn't wait and needed to see the world beyond his bedroom walls. Jack looked at his brother's reflection in the mirror. He certainly looked older than his thirteen years and that worried Jack, who did not want his kid brother to follow in his footsteps and start visiting pubs and clubs underage. He had seen what it could do and he himself was no exception. It wasn't just the beer, but that was the start; it could and almost certainly did lead on to things of a more serious nature. He checked his wallet making sure his money was all there as he would need his wage packet to get what he wanted. He saved whatever he could from his job at his uncle's grocery shop; it didn't pay very much but it was enough to keep him going.

'Ok, how do I look?'

He turned round, showing his young brother his going-out look. Ben ran his eye over his brother and inspected him from head to foot. The button-down collar of his light blue shirt with a darker sleeveless jumper looked good with his navy flared trousers and brown Chelsea boots. To Ben's eyes he looked amazing.

'You'll do,' he said as he picked a cotton thread that had attached itself to Jack's jumper.

Jack felt good and ready to go. He smiled at his brother. 'Soon, Ben, soon, and remember what I always say – never make a promise you can't keep.'

Ben watched as his brother went down the stairs. He heard him say goodbye to their mum and her telling Jack to be home at a reasonable time and not to get into trouble. Jack had become the head of the household since their father had died in a stupid traffic accident two years before, and although he tried to look after his mother and brother, he found it difficult. Both boys missed their dad and could see the devastating effect it had on their mother. She had managed somehow to get through that terrible period of her life and keep the boys out of harm's way. The boys got a lot of help from their mum's brother, uncle Steven. He had given Jack a job in his greengrocer's business when he left school and treated him well. Steven was very fond of his nephews, not having any children of his own, and he and his wife had learnt to live with the fact that other people's children would have to do.

Something woke Ben – a shout followed by a scream. He sat bolt upright in bed then heard another scream. It was his mum. He jumped up and ran to his bedroom door; now the screaming was non-stop. He felt sick and scared but fuelled with adrenalin as he ran down the stairs. He saw his mother at the front door with two policemen.

'What have you done to my mum!' Ben shouted as he reached the foot of the stairs.

'Steady, boy, we haven't done anything to your mum.'

Ben's mum turned and grabbed him, seeming to lose all control as one minute she was sobbing and the next screaming. Ben didn't know what to do and looked up pleadingly at one of the policemen.

'What's wrong? What's happened?

The constable saw the look of dread in the boy's face. 'Let's get your mum inside.' Ben put an arm round his mother's shoulders, guided her into the front room and sat her down on the settee, the policeman sitting in the chair opposite. He clasped his mother's hand tightly and waited for the policeman to speak. The constable drew in a deep breath.

'It's about your brother.'

'What about Jack? He was fine when he left home.'

The constable continued, 'There has been an incident and I'm afraid Jack was involved. He was taken to the hospital where the doctors did all they could, but they were unable to save him.'

'You mean – he's dead?' Ben started to shake. He could not and would not believe Jack was dead. 'You're lying – he just went to a club for a night out.'

'What's your name?' the policeman asked.

'Ben,' he replied.

'Well, Ben, I'm afraid that sadly your brother passed away this evening.' Ben shuddered again and shook his head.

The policeman turned to Ben's mother. 'Is there anyone we can call to come over?'

She couldn't speak and just stared numbly into the fireplace. Ben found his voice and spoke for her. 'Could you contact our uncle Steven? He's on the phone – I'll get his number.'

Their uncle had had a phone installed for emergencies after their father had died, and Ben was glad he had.

The day became a blur as police moved around the house. Ben's uncle arrived within ten minutes of the police contacting him. Fortunately, he only lived a mile or so away. His arrival set his sister off again and she sat huddled into herself on the sofa, moaning and sobbing in turn. Consoling her was almost impossible, no matter how gentle he was.

Steven turned to look at Ben. 'Are the school going to be concerned about you not turning up in the morning?'

Ben replied without hesitation, 'They can think what they like. Mum needs me here and that's where I'm going to be until she is better and I get to know what's going on.'

Steven looked at his nephew and realised how much he seemed to have grown up in a couple of hours. The lad had a stern look on his face, and although the tracks of tears could be seen on his cheeks he had pulled himself together and was now in control of his emotions. Steven told him not to worry. 'We can talk to your school tomorrow.'

A few minutes later the doorbell rang again and another policeman entered, this time in plain clothes. After a brief chat with the uniformed officer, he turned to Steven and asked if it was alright to take a look at Jack's bedroom. Seeing the policeman going up the stairs, Ben got up from beside his mum and followed.

'What are you doing? There's nothing in there but our stuff.'

Turning to face him, the police officer said, 'We have to search your brother's things as there may be something that will help us find out what happened to him and why.'

'What are you looking for? I'm telling you there's nothing to be found.'

As he said it, one of the policemen stood up from crouching beside Jack's bed and held out a screw of paper containing what looked to be a number of tablets. 'This is what we're looking for. Do you know anything about your brother's habits, especially taking stuff like this?'

Ben shook his head. He had no idea what pills his brother might have been taking. Innocently he said, 'Perhaps they're for headaches or something.'

'I think your brother may have been taking them for something rather more than headaches.' The policeman shook his head and muttered something under his breath. 'Tell me, do you know where your brother went on Friday evenings?'

Ben told the truth. 'He went to clubs up town. He liked to dance and listen to the music and see if he could find himself a girlfriend.'

'Do you know the names of any of the clubs he went to?'

Ben couldn't think straight, but one name came to mind. 'He did tell me that his favourite was a club called 'The Painted Door', and I think it was in Earls Court.'

'Do you know if that's where he was going last night?'

'No, sorry, he only said he was going clubbing.'

The detective could see that the boy was feeling the pressure so he said kindly, 'Why don't you go and see your mum and uncle and I'll let you know if I need your help again. Listen, thanks for what you've told me, it's a great help.'

Ben went down the stairs and into the front room where he saw his mother with her head down being talked to gently by his uncle. He collapsed into an armchair. An uneasy atmosphere could be felt in the room. The police were moving around and talking to each other in lowered voices.

One of the officers looked up. 'We will need to take formal statements, I'm afraid. It shouldn't take long and we may be able to fill in some of the details we need to help discover what happened to Jack.'

Steven asked, 'Does that include the boy?'

The policeman looked at Ben sympathetically. 'Everyone connected with Jack needs to give us any information they have that might help with our enquiries.'

'My sister is not in a fit state to do anything at the moment. Can it wait till she's in a better state of mind?'

The officer looked at his colleague, who nodded. 'Could you bring her to the station tomorrow with your nephew?'

Steven still had his arm around his sister's shoulders. 'I'll do my best.'

The police left the house. Although they hadn't been there long, the shock of what they had imparted left Ben, his mother, and his uncle stunned. Ben closed his eyes and could see Jack as he left for his night out, all smartly kitted up. He remembered what his brother had said – never make promises you can't keep. Ben thought long and hard and made a promise to take it upon himself to find out who had killed his brother – and god help them when he did.

The sun shone on the day Jack was buried. All of Ben's family were there, his uncle and aunt supporting his mother, who was still in a very bad way. The church of St Michael's stood grey in the light of the late morning. The service was short; Ben's uncle Steven said some kind words, but to Ben no words could ever describe his brother's short life. Jack was interred next to his father. A headstone lay by the side of the grave ready to be erected following the funeral. It was plain, just the details of his name, and date of birth and death in simple lettering. Ben took a handful of soil and let it drop onto the coffin. As he looked down, he said to himself that one day he would make those responsible for his brother's death pay. 'Sleep easy, brother,' he whispered. He put his arm round his mother and helped lead her back to the black limousine.

The months following the funeral were stressful. Nothing seemed to go right for Ben and his family. The coroner's verdict was one of misadventure, which Ben did not think right. Although he had no experience of drugs, he could not understand why Jack would do something so crazy. The police had told the family that they couldn't get to the bottom of the case as the use of uppers and downers, purple hearts and things like speed, were hard to trace to an individual, and their job was even harder now that more dangerous drugs such as heroin, cocaine, and something called LSD were appearing on the streets and in the clubs. These, the drugs of the wealthy, were now becoming available, at a price, to the club-goers of London. This didn't mean very much to Ben; he believed with all his heart that Jack wouldn't do that sort of thing.

His mother seemed to lose the will to do anything. She would sit in her armchair clutching two photos, one of Jack and one of her husband. There were no tears falling from her eyes, just blankness, nothingness. All emotion was dead. Ben and his uncle did all they could to bring her out of her depression but had little success. The only response they were able to get was when they offered her a cup of tea. She accepted tea, but ate nothing.

As the days passed, she became weaker, and eventually they had no option but to call their doctor, who explained to Ben and his uncle that in his opinion they needed to get her to hospital. The doctor had told Ben's uncle that she needed psychiatric help, which meant nothing to Ben, but if that was what was needed, then so be it.

His uncle continued to keep an eye on his nephew and took him to visit his mother as often as he could, but it broke Ben's heart to see his mum in such a state, especially as he could see no improvement. As she slowly deteriorated, he felt he was losing his world. Eventually she contracted pneumonia, and sadly didn't have the energy or will to fight it.

Ben's life was in turmoil and he could not focus on anything. His schoolwork went by the board, and although he looked after the house as well as he could, he could not concentrate on the simplest of things. His mother's condition took a downward turn and two weeks after being admitted, her body gave out and she died, not in physical pain but in the mental agony of losing her husband and son; everything she had suffered finally took its toll.

The loss of Jack was a blow which Ben thought he would never recover from, but his mother leaving him as well was just too much to bear. He fell into a dream-world of pain and horror, tormented by the picture of his brother in his head and never able to understand or believe that his brother would do something so stupid as to take pills that could kill him. It was only the care and attention of his uncle that kept him on the right side of sanity.

His mother's funeral took place in the same church as his brother's, and those that attended were friends of the family, two of Steven's colleagues, and some of the neighbours who had known Ben's mother well. Her grave was next to her son's and her husband's. Ben stood back and looked at the three headstones. He felt faint, his legs no longer able to support him, and if it hadn't been for his uncle and aunt he would have collapsed. He managed to bend and grasp a handful of earth and sprinkle it gently onto his mother's coffin, just as he had so recently done at his brother's. His only thoughts were that someone should be held accountable for their deaths. They turned and left the churchyard with heavy hearts.

Steven had seen his family destroyed and did everything he could to help Ben through this hell. He gently coaxed him into agreeing to move in with him and his wife and to carry on at school. Ben knew that if it wasn't for his uncle, he might well have gone the same way as his mum. It took a great deal of time and patience.

Steven had a business to run, but he took Ben under his wing and encouraged him to think about his future and what he would like to do with his life. Ben had an idea that wasn't exactly high flying in 1966. He didn't want to be another Bobby Moore or Geoff Hurst like most of the lads in their final year at school, nor did the idea of an apprenticeship in some factory appeal to him. When he had moved in with his uncle, he had decided he could at least make himself useful. His Aunt Sarah agreed reluctantly that he could earn his keep by cooking for her and his uncle. So Ben decided he would use everything he had learnt from his mother, and together with a variety of cook books, would become their very own chef.

It was not only cooking that Ben contributed to the running of the house – he also helped his uncle collect vegetables from Covent Garden market. This meant very early starts, but it was worth it as Ben picked up a lot of useful information about where vegetables came from and to some extent even how to cook them. His most important discovery was from one of his uncle's customers, an elderly Italian gentleman who took a shine to him. They had long discussions on the food of Italy and how to prepare it. At one point his aunt became concerned when Ben started to use olive oil to cook with, as in her experience it was normally bought from a chemist to help people with sunburn or to clear ear wax. His uncle had to put her mind at rest by explaining that the British had a lot of catching up to do as far as cooking went, and olive oil was part of something called the Mediterranean diet that was becoming popular.

Steven watched the boy as his keen sense of smell and taste led to some very interesting dishes. Ben finally discussed the idea of becoming a chef with him, and Steven agreed to help him find the right path to take if he was serious. As his final days at school approached, Ben was convinced his chosen career lay in the kitchen.

Steven supplied a London hotel with vegetables from various countries and had got to know the head chef quite well. He asked if there was any chance of Ben getting a place in his kitchen.

'Let me see the lad. If I think he has the passion you need to become a chef, I might be able to take him on, but no promises.'

Steven was very grateful, and an interview was arranged. When he gave him the news, Ben just hugged his uncle with a gratitude never before expressed.

2

Steven arranged for Ben to meet David Burdett, the head chef of the Rosegarth, a very upmarket five-star hotel in Belgravia. His uncle had bought him a new suit and he had his hair cut in the college-boy style, which made him look very smart, as his aunt Sarah kept telling him. The meeting had been arranged for a Tuesday morning at ten o'clock, which was apparently a quiet time in the kitchens. When Ben arrived, he didn't know where to go, so he took the bull by the horns and decided that reception was the most likely place. He felt totally intimidated, in part by the staff, who looked smart and efficient, but also by the sheer opulence of the hotel. It was decorated in a modern style and had all the elegance appropriate to its five stars. As he started to pull open the door a bell boy stopped him.

'Where do you think you're going?' It was the voice of a trumped-up little puppet.

Ben explained quietly that he had a meeting arranged with Mr Burdett, the head chef.

'In that case I suppose you'd better come in.' He looked down his nose at Ben as he opened the door. 'See the receptionist and she will get someone to take you to the kitchen.'

Ben thought that if the kitchen staff were as ignorant as that little prat he would have his work cut out getting along with people.

The receptionist, however, was more approachable, and very efficient, and when Ben had given her his details, she phoned the kitchen. After a brief conversation the receptionist called another bell boy to escort Ben to Mr Burdett's office. As he walked behind the boy his nerves started to get the better of him, but he knew he had to remain in control as his future depended on him getting this job. His escort knocked on an office door which was opened by a man dressed in chef's whites.

'Ben Croxley to see you, Mr Burdett.' The bell boy tipped his head as Mr Burdett held out his hand to greet Ben.

'Come in, Ben, and sit down. Your uncle tells me you want to be a chef. What I would like to hear from you is why.' Ben tried hard to think how to reply but his thoughts got confused. David Burdett could see he was finding it difficult to explain, so he added, 'Tell me, what was the last thing you cooked and why you cooked it.' Ben felt a lot easier – this was something he could talk about.

'I cooked a meal for my aunt and uncle last night. I try to make things a little different each time I'm in the kitchen. I'd bought a chicken and cut it into manageable pieces. The day before, I'd been to the market with my uncle and I had some fresh herbs, so I chopped the thyme, oregano, and some rosemary very finely, added two cloves of garlic and mixed them in some olive oil.' Here Ben's enthusiasm really took over. 'I tried to dry the chicken as best I could and then marinated it in the herbs and oil for an hour. While I was waiting, I made a mixture of vegetables – that's some potatoes, courgettes, an aubergine and tomatoes. I seasoned them and put them to one side.'

Burdett smiled to himself and wondered if he should stop the boy there, but he sat back in his chair and tried to look captivated by Ben's detailed explanation.

'I selected the chicken breasts, mainly because that's my aunt's favourite, then placed them in a pot with a covering of stock ready for the oven.' Ben drew a breath, but before Burdett could call a halt he continued, 'The veg went in to cook with a few sprigs of thyme and rosemary. I knew that the chicken would cook quite quickly and I wanted to make sure everything was finished together. The chicken went into the oven next and I got on with the washing up. I had to make sure the veg was just coloured but not burnt. I checked the chicken didn't dry out and it all came together nicely. My aunt and uncle seemed to enjoy it, which was what I was aiming for.'

David Burdett leaned back. He liked not only what Ben had described, but the way he went through the process and how his enthusiasm spilled over so much he couldn't keep his hands still, which showed him that this boy just loved to cook.

He smiled at Ben. 'You know that the kitchen is not a place for skivers and wimps and that it's bloody hard work?' Ben winced a bit but said that he was fully aware he would be worked very hard. David Burdett started to explain to Ben just what he would be required to do.

'You will start where everyone starts – at the bottom. Your job will be cleaning all the pots, pans, utensils, grills, ovens, and anything else that's been used. You will have to be quick, but careful hygiene is top priority in my kitchen and if any customer of the hotel goes down with food poisoning, god help the person responsible.' He paused, then added, 'If you're successful in coming to work for me, I will tell you now that the money is poor and the hours long. It would mean a 50-hour week, some early starts, some late finishes, on a basic wage of £17 a week. Overtime does not come into it – we all work until the service has been completed.'

Ben looked at his possible future boss and didn't know quite how to take him. Burdett seemed to be a man who wanted anyone who worked for him to understand what was required of them, and, although appearing friendly enough, was not a person to be taken lightly. Neither would he take kindly to fools. Ben glanced around the office. He could see that the books on the shelves behind Burdett's desk were all to do with cooking and food, ranging from books by Elizabeth David to something called Nouvelle Cuisine, something new to Ben.

'Whoever works for me starts as an escuelerie – a plongeur. Both mean the same – dishwasher. Getting to know the language of the kitchen is half the battle!' he said with a laugh.

Ben felt a little deflated at the thought of being a dishwasher, but soon bucked up when Burdett went on to tell him that if he proved his worth, he could progress through the ranks of the kitchen brigade once he had gained the required knowledge.

Burdett went on to say that although the hours were unsocial, it would be in his interest to go part-time to college and get his City & Guilds certificates in Food Preparation & Cooking as these would stand him in good stead for promotion. Burdett finished the interview by asking if Ben had any questions. He said he had only one, that if he got the job was there anywhere for him to keep his bike?

Burdett smiled. 'I'm sure a secure place can be found for a bike.' With that he stood. Ben jumped up, not knowing how to say goodbye, but it wasn't a problem as Burdett held out his hand and Ben shook it. Burdett's grip was vice-like and Ben thought he would not like to get on the wrong side of him.

It was two days later that Ben received a letter offering him a job in the kitchens at the Rosegarth. It set out the hours of work and the pay; Ben winced when he saw how small the amount was, but he could manage, he would have to. That night he sat with his uncle and discussed the job offer. His uncle asked if he really thought this was the career he wanted because he was not going to get rich quick. Ben said he didn't mind as long as he could see a path that might lead to something better. He asked his uncle what the 'probationary' period of three months meant.

'That's to see if you fit in with them and they fit in with you. It's a standard clause in any job offer.'

Ben thought for a moment. 'Does that mean they can fire me easily during the first three months?'

Steven put on his serious face. 'Well, you may find that you can't fit in with the routine or staff in the kitchen, and on the other hand they may not think you're up to the job, so yes, the first three months are important to both you and the kitchen.'

Ben nodded. 'So it's do or die in the probationary period.'

Steven could see a wave of concern cross his face. 'Ben, you can do it if you really want the job. Now, there is something else we need to talk about,' He looked serious. 'When your father passed away there was an insurance claim of a considerable amount. It was not just life insurance, it was also a claim made against the company of the vehicle involved in the accident. The lorry had defective brakes and the pay-out was enough to buy the house your parents were renting. When your mother died, the house passed on to you. I have been looking after it along with two other properties I currently own. All three properties are rented out. When you become twenty-one the house becomes yours. Until then I am responsible for its upkeep and income. The income goes into a trust fund which you will also have access to when you reach twenty-one. Up until then, if you need any funding, I will advance you money from my own account. Is there anything in particular you need to start this job?

Ben took a breath. 'I've had a look at the distance to the Rosegarth and know that I could easily use my bike to get there and back, but my bike is not in the best of condition.'

Steven looked at his nephew. 'So you need a new bike.'

'Yes, 'cos it would be a disaster if my bike collapsed on me on the way to work and made me late.'

Steven smiled. 'Tomorrow is Saturday. If you can wait till I have finished, around one o'clock, we will get go and get you a new bike.'

Ben was thrilled. 'That's great! Thanks, Uncle Steven, I promise I won't let you down.'

3

Although a dishwasher had a fancy name, escuelerie, Ben soon learnt that it was very hard work. And that his pay packet wasn't great. Still, it was the path he had chosen, and with determination and guts he would make it work. He started his three-month probationary period on an early shift, 8am to 6pm. He wasn't alone as another new starter worked alongside him. His name was Rodger and he was the same age as Ben. Fortunately, they hit it off, and at the end of their first three months they made a pact that they would drag each other through the bad times and make sure they both succeeded in the kitchen.

The hours were long and the work sweaty and punishing. Late starts led to very late finishes and cycling home was not a joy at one in the morning. Ben's life fell into a routine with the kitchen the place where he spent most of his waking hours. One thing about Burdett was that he insisted staff took breaks, whether it was for a smoke or just to get some air into their lungs. He said to all he wanted his staff to be able to work in his kitchen, not lie in a hospital bed after stupid accidents due to tiredness.

Everyone in the kitchen looked haggard after a full shift. Some would turn to alcohol and Ben suspected some would turn to drugs to keep them going. All those in the kitchen from kitchen assistants to the chef de cuisine, had begun their careers at Ben's level and they knew how thankless and tiring the role was. A high turnover due to burnout, accident, or problems with various substances made Ben aware of the risks and opportunities the kitchen held.

The days passed, however. It was a relief when Burdett from time to time picked one of the staff to prepare a dish, and that included Ben and Rodger, which put them in the spotlight. They were treated the same as anybody else and the criticism was harsh. Ben and Rodger encouraged each other and discussed how to improve what they cooked.

An event that changed both their lives occurred when a sous chef decided to leave and take his friend, a chef de partie, with him. This resulted in a shift in the kitchen. On the Sunday after their jobs had been completed, Burdett called both Ben and Rodger into his office.

'You know we are losing two good members of the brigade, which means I have gaps to fill.' Ben and Rodger nodded and glanced at each other wide-eyed. 'I need two replacement commis chefs. You two have shown your worth in the kitchen, so do you think you're ready for a step up?'

They answered in unison. 'Yes, we're ready!'

Burdett looked at them sternly. 'I'm giving you a chance to show what you're capable of, so don't let me down.'

'We won't, Chef!'

He looked from one to the other. 'You've only been with the hotel for nine months, but I reckon if I put my faith in you, you will prove me right.' Burdett felt confident he was doing the right thing; both had worked hard and kept their noses clean, but most importantly they had fitted into the team well. 'Next shift, you will start as commis chefs. This means, as you will already know, you spend at least two months on each station and learn how each section works. You will be under a chef de partie, who will let me know how you get on as you move around. Get yourselves some fresh whites and be ready for some hard graft. Any questions? No? Then good luck to you.'

Life moved on a pace after their promotion and it seemed that the gods were looking kindly upon them. As they worked under different chefs de partie, they learnt the ways of the kitchen starting with preparation, butchery, fish filleting, pastry making, and a lot more. Much of it was pure repetition but it made them proficient in what they were called upon to do. The going was tough and the pressure great, and abuse flew from the mouths of those wanting to get their plates to the customers. Ben and Rodger somehow kept each other going. The drudgery of cycling to work was compensated by Ben's love of what he did. He enjoyed the range of learning at different stations and as he made pastry, cut up chickens, prepared joints for the sous chefs, he dreamed about how he would one day have a kitchen of his own.

The Rosegarth was a hotel with a reputation for fine dining, and being surrounded by embassies and consulates they were required to produce a very varied menu. Ben discovered that the owner of the hotel was a powerful head of state in the far east. Rodger's best guess was the Sultan of Brunei, but Ben thought it might be one of the sheiks from the middle east, perhaps Oman. whoever it was they were very wealthy and paid their wages, so they were happy.

Occasionally the kitchen was called upon to do some outside catering and it surprised Ben when Burdett asked him if he would like to assist him in catering for a dinner party. Ben felt honoured and grabbed at a chance to work alongside his boss. Burdett gave him the basic details of what would be required and that it would mean a few extra pounds in his wage packet. It was a selective dinner party for a long-standing customer of the hotel who, for reasons of his own, was organising a get-together of some business colleagues. It would be a very private gathering and Ben would be needed in the kitchen, but that was all. Ben asked who the customer was, and was told he was a man who had made a great deal of money in developing properties and establishing nightclubs, together with a string of discotheques. He also told Ben, rather grimly, 'He's a very wealthy man but he also likes to tell his stories about how he started out, so if he corners you, be aware he will bore you stupid with tales of his rise to fortune and power.'

Rodger was a little put out when he heard that Ben had been selected to help the boss, but he took a stoic approach to Ben's good fortune.

The kitchen carried on apace, and both Ben and Rodger proved to be good investments. The head chef was pleased with the feedback he was getting from the chefs the boys prepped for.

'Tomorrow morning we are going to visit the customer, so best bib and tucker, Ben.'

'What exactly do you want me to do?' Ben asked a little apprehensively.

'I want you to shadow me and only speak when you're spoken to.'

Ben thought that seemed easy enough. 'What time do you want me here?'

'Nine-thirty would be good. The Rosegarth is not far from the customer's house and our meeting is at ten.'

Ben caught the tube to work that morning, not wanting to cycle in his best trousers and jacket. He arrived five minutes early and Burdett was waiting for him and talked him through what would happen.

'We will be offered tea or coffee when we arrive. Please yourself on that but don't spill anything! The house is a Georgian terrace and in this part of London that means a great deal of money, so make sure you wipe your feet.' Burdett told Ben he was going to suggest a menu that would centre on Beef Wellington. He had already discussed the menu with the hotel sommelier, so was able to recommend several wines. 'Once I have firmed up the menu with the customer, I'll take you to the kitchen. I've been there before. It's not an enormous place but it is very well fitted out. All you will need are your knives. It will only take us fifteen minutes so we will walk to his house.'

As they walked, Burdett asked Ben what he wanted to do with his life. Ben explained that he would like to get to the top of the tree and hopefully get a place of his own. Burdett smiled; it was the wish of most young chefs. Many tried but few succeeded. He then asked Ben about his college work and Ben admitted it was hard going, working in the hotel plus day-release at college, but he was enjoying it.

'What level are you studying for?'

'It's level two and I have my final exam next week.'

Burdett had lost track of how far Ben had progressed. 'You know, you should start to think about a possible placement in the not-too-distant future. Come and see me when you get your results.' Ben was not expecting that and felt a surge of anticipation well up through his body.

'Here we are.'

Ben's gaze ran over the front of the house, taking in the very impressive stone steps that led up from the pavement to an immaculate front door. Painted black, with brass furniture, it gleamed in the sunlight. Burdett rang the bell, and for a minute or two they could hear nothing until the door was opened by a ramrod-straight woman carrying a duster like a staff of office.

'Yes?' Her tone was one of indifference.

'We have an appointment with Mr Steyning.'

Impassive, she asked, 'Who shall I say is calling?'

Burdett seemed a little bemused. 'David Burdett from the Rosegarth.'

'And who's this?' She pointed her duster at Ben's chest.

'This is my assistant, Ben Croxley.'

She favoured them with a frosty look. 'Come in – and take your shoes off.'

They did as they were told; leaving a mark anywhere in that house would be tantamount to a capital crime. Ben followed his boss up the staircase to the next floor. It was jaw-dropping, the way the light cascaded down from a magnificent landing window picking up the patterns of the richly-hued carpet; it must have cost a fortune. The banister rail was of dark wood that stood out against the smooth white walls. He had never seen anything quite so grand – it was what dreams were made of.

'Expensive,' Ben muttered glancing at Burdett. 'He must be worth a few bob.'

'And the rest.' Burdett looked around at some new pieces of furniture he had not seen on his previous visit; they alone would have cost a packet. The hotel enjoyed expensive fittings and fixtures, but this was a private house! Money just dripped off the gilded mirrors. A door to the right of the hallway opened and a man of medium height and build appeared. His walk was purposeful and confident and his small sharp eyes appraised his visitors. Ben could see his suit was expensive, probably wool, and definitely not 'off the peg'. It was patterned in a fine check, and his light blue shirt with a red silk tie and a glint of gold on his wrist, completed an air of wealth and power.

'We meet again.' Steyning held out his hand towards Burdett. As they shook hands he looked towards Ben. 'Who's this?'

'This is my assistant,' Burdett replied. 'He will be helping me prepare the meal.'

'His name is?'

'Sorry, this is Ben Croxley. Ben – Mr Steyning.'

'Pleased to meet you, Ben.' Turning back to Burdett he added, 'Shall we get on?'

Steyning led them into a lavishly furnished drawing room.

'Take a seat.' They sank into one of the sofas. It was Steyning who started the conversation. 'I have some unfortunate news to start with. The meal that was planned for two weeks' time has changed and is now scheduled to take place in six weeks' time. Does that present any problems for you?'

Burdett looked across at Steyning. 'I'll have to check our diary, of course, but I can't see any difficulties in re-arranging things.' Steyning looked pleased.

'Ok, so now let's get down to the nitty gritty. What sort of menu are you suggesting, bearing in mind that my guests would like something British?'

Burdett opened the plastic folder he was carrying and passed a hand-written menu to Steyning. 'Hors d'oeuvres would take the form of a dish of crudités – in other words a selection of fine raw vegetables with dipping sauces. This would be followed by a fish course of Sole Meunière with Beef Wellington as the main.'

Steyning nodded. 'Sounds good so far. What about dessert?'

'After the richness of the Wellington I thought something a little light – perhaps a pistachio soufflé with pistachio ice cream.'

'Now that sounds delicious.' Steyning looked approvingly at the draft menu.

'You did say to keep it to four courses,' continued Burdett, 'and I have tried to give you variety but keeping to a British centre with the Wellington.' He had hoped this would fit the bill, and by Steyning's reaction it had. 'If you are in agreement, I will get the menu printed for your guests to study and possibly keep as a souvenir of the evening.'

Steyning seemed satisfied and stood up. 'Thanks for the menu. It looks good and I'm sorry for any inconvenience with the dates. If you could let me see the final menu, I would be grateful.'

'Once I've got it printed, I'll send Ben with it, and if you have any further requirements or there are any changes, you can let him know – we can accommodate most things.'

They made their way to the front door and put their shoes on under the dour gaze of the housekeeper. Once outside, Ben asked how Steyning got his money. Burdett looked at him with a sardonic smile. 'Some things you just don't ask about. I would advise you not to go down that road, you never know what you might meet.'

Ben nodded his understanding; he would not pry, although he was certainly curious.

4

L ife in the kitchen continued at its usual busy pace, with Ben and Rodger continuing to learn their trade. New things seemed to appear every day. They both took the pressure in their stride and even the boring bits took on a challenge.

Two days after his visit to Steyning, Ben caught sight of an attractive figure passing by his work station. She was a petite, well-shaped girl with brown hair and deep brown eyes. It was one of those occasions that, as he looked at her and she at him and they smiled at each other, that said they would both like to know each other better. Rodger noticed what had passed between them.

'You're in there,' he said with a broad grin.

Ben blushed. 'What do you mean? I don't even know her name.'

'That's easily remedied,' replied Rodger, giving his mate a friendly punch. 'Her name is Sophie and she is unattached – although there are quite a few who'd like to know her better!'

Ben carried on cleaning his station but held a picture of the girl in his mind. *Sophie*, he thought, nice name. He shook his head and carried on with his work.

Later, Ben was given the amended menu to take to Steyning for approval and sign off. When he reached the house he felt a little scared, but couldn't have said why. He rang the bell and was greeted by the same haughty woman, still holding her duster like a weapon. She snapped at him, 'Come in, he's in the drawing room – and take your shoes off.'

Ben did as ordered, and clutching the menu went towards the drawing room. He knocked on the door and Steyning's voice called out sharply, 'Come in!' Opening the door, Ben could see Steyning sitting at a desk. 'Ah Ben, come in take a seat, I'll be with you in a minute.'

Ben watched while this wealthy individual sorted through some papers, signing one and scoring things out on another.

'Have you got the new menu?'

Ben reached forward and handed it over. Steyning studied it and made a noise of agreement. He picked up his expensive-looking pen again and signed across the bottom of the menu.

'There you go,' he said, handing it back to Ben. 'How long have you been at the hotel?'

Ben was a little perturbed that Steyning should ask him questions. 'I've been there nearly two years.'

'And what do you want to do with your life?'

'I want to be a good chef and one day hopefully own my own restaurant.'

Steyning considered this. 'When I was your age I wanted the world and I was prepared to work for it.' Ben remembered he had been warned about Steyning's love of blowing his own trumpet but was willing to let him carry on. 'I started with very little and worked my way up from the bottom – and look what I have now!' He waved his hand around the room. 'Very impressive, don't you think?'

'Very,' Ben agreed. He thought for a moment and decided he would ask a question and see where it took the conversation. 'I guess it was hard work? What sort of business were you in?'

'The entertainment business.' Steyning's voice rose a little and he sat up in his chair – Ben could sense that he was about to get the full life-story. 'I started working in one of the clubs as a teenager doing odd jobs, cleaning, running errands, fetching and carrying until I could prove myself a valuable asset to my employer.' Apparently, it hadn't taken Steyning long before he was part of the booking team that arranged for acts to appear at the clubs he worked for. He continued, 'It was long hours. I had to make sure that everything went without a hitch. That included the acts and all the public who crammed into the club.'

Ben became a little more interested. 'What sort of clubs were they?' Steyning glanced around at the photos on his wall. 'They were clubs where youngsters could dance the night away … do you know, those kids could dance 'til dawn and still go to work!'

Ben chuckled. 'There's no way I could do that! I'm knackered just working, let alone going out in the evening. What were the names of your clubs?'

'Not my clubs then – they belonged to my bosses. There were quite a few different names as sometimes we had to shut down fairly quickly for various reasons. One of my favourites was the 'Painted Door'– that was my first rung on the management ladder.'

Ben was getting very interested. 'I was wondering – did you have any problems with the customers staying awake? Because if it was me I'd be asleep on my feet.'

'Ah well, we did have certain things that would help keep them going.'

Ben thought, *in for a penny, in for a pound.* 'What sort of things?'

Steyning was by now in full flow. 'Uppers and downers,

pills to pop for very little money, but they would keep the punters happy and wanting to return to the club.'

'Wasn't that dangerous?' Ben realised that might not be the right thing to ask, but Steyning carried on.

'In all my time we only had one serious problem. Some stupid kid took more than he could handle and his heart gave out. But I was able to sort it out and the police came to the conclusion it was his own fault.' Ben felt very cold yet his palms were sweaty. 'But that's a long time ago.' He looked at his watch. 'God, is that the time? I've got to make some phone calls. Have you got all you want, young man?'

Ben picked up the menu and nodded. 'Yes, thanks.'

Steyning turned and lifted the phone and Ben made his way back to the front door. As he walked back to the hotel, he reflected on what Steyning had said, and a vague misgiving started in his brain about a possible connection between Steyning's link to clubs and his brother's death.'

*

Ben's uneasiness tailed off rapidly as the weather took a turn for the good and the temperature rose. He continued on his bike, taking the easiest way into work. His route took him through some of the better parts of London, and he dreamt of living in one of the amazing Georgian and Victorian properties he passed. The roads he took had names that initially meant nothing, except to those living nearby, until he came to the Hammersmith Road which conjured up the Palais de Danse and the fun and games that were had in there. Then the really posh names came into view – Kensington High Street and Knightsbridge, which took him to the heart of Belgravia and to his place of work. It wasn't the shortest route, but he enjoyed it in the sun (and hated it in the rain and snow).

He jumped off his bike and placed it next to Rodger's, which looked decidedly tatty against his own.

As he walked towards the kitchen entrance, the girl, Sophie, came out of the door. They both stopped and awkwardly tried to pass each other. He could smell her perfume, light and flowery and not too powerful like some of the waitresses used'.

'Could you give me a hand?' she asked. Her voice was soft, but held a firmness of purpose. He could detect no strong accent, although a London drawl was in there somewhere.

'Sure, what do you want me to do?' He felt a blush creeping up his face and wished he knew how to stop it.

'It's just the fresh linen – I need to get it to the dining room.'

He looked at the pile of tablecloths and thought he could manage them with a little help from her. She took the first half dozen and he lifted the rest. As they turned to head towards the dining room their arms brushed each other and a feeling of excitement tingled through his body. Now it was her turn to blush. He didn't know what to say or do, so he stuttered, 'Have you worked here long?' thinking *what a stupid question.*

She smiled at him. 'About as long as you have.' *How does she know how long I've worked here?* 'I've seen you going in and out of the kitchen but I don't think you noticed me,' she said coyly.

Ben gazed at the tablecloths as if they might inspire him with something sensible to say. 'I suppose your hours are the same as mine?'

'I suppose so.' They both hoped the conversation would last a bit longer, but what could they say to each other? He took the bull by the horns.

'What time do you start?'

'I get here about 9 o'clock when I'm on earlies and about 3 when I'm on lates. What about you?'

'A bit earlier for me – about 8 on earlies and about 1 on lates.'

'Do you ever have coffee before you start?'

Ben never had coffee before he started. He coughed. 'Not usually, but if a special occasion came up I'm sure I could manage a cup.'

'What shift are you on?'

He sighed. 'I'm on earlies, so it would have to be after my shift.'

Sophie smiled. 'That's ok, I'm on earlies as well. What time do you think you would be finished?'

Ben was not thinking that clearly but he managed to get things into perspective. 'It won't be until 6 and I don't know if the café will be open at that time.'

Sophie looked at him, wondering if he was worth the effort. She decided he was. 'Shall we say we'll meet up at 6:15 tomorrow? If you're not there I can always start without you!'

Ben stammered that he would do his best. *Bloody hell,* he thought, *what is happening here?* He liked her but had only known her for a few minutes. Still, don't let opportunities pass you by, he figured. 'Yes, that would be good. I'll see you then.'

He couldn't believe what had just happened. He smiled at her as they put the tablecloths down, and continued to smile rather smugly to himself as he made his way back to the kitchen.

Rodger had seen Ben talking to Sophie. 'You sly dog, I didn't know you had it in you.'

Ben blushed again; god, he was getting sick of this inability to control his habit of getting red in the face.

'It's only for a cup of coffee.'

Rodger winked. 'That's what you say.' They both laughed and went into the kitchen.

5

The day was gloomy and overcast but it was not raining so that was something in its favour. Ben made his way to a small café, the nearest one to the hotel, with three tables squeezed onto the pavement outside its main window. It was nothing posh, just a place where you could get a cup of coffee and a croissant or a bacon sarnie. Ben went in and looked round for Sophie but couldn't see her. He was a little early so he ordered a cappuccino and took it to a table near the door. The owner of the café was a jack of all trades; he did everything from working the coffee machine to cooking an all-day English breakfast. Ben watched as he moved swiftly from one job to another and wondered what the man would be like in his kitchen – *different worlds*, he thought. The door opened and Sophie spotted him straightaway.

'Am I late?' she asked breathlessly.

'No, you're bang on time, I'm the one who's early. What can I get you?'

Sophie looked down at Ben's cup. 'That looks good, I'll have the same.'

Ben got up and went to the counter. 'Another cappuccino, please.'

Wiping his hands on his apron the owner beamed at him. 'No problem, I'll bring it over.' He liked the look of this young couple and smiled to himself; *young love.*

Sophie sat down and looked across at Ben, who had the feeling that he was being assessed as he felt Sophie's eyes wander all over his face. She observed small details about his appearance; his hair was not as neat as when they met in the hotel, but he had ridden to work on his bike and just finished a shift, so that was expected. His face was clean-shaven with eyebrows so blond as to be almost indistinguishable, and his blue eyes were piercing as he looked at her. He had a tan from his bike riding, which Sophie thought made him rather attractive, so yes, on the whole, quite a nice-looking guy.

She underwent the same treatment from Ben as he looked at this girl who he didn't know anything about, and watched the way she took her first sips of coffee, leaving a white foam moustache on her top lip. He gestured to her and she realised what he was trying to indicate. She wiped away the foam and smiled; she had a lovely gentle smile. Her hair framed the oval shape of her face in a sort of bob. Although Ben wasn't quite sure what it was called, he liked it.

'I don't know much about you,' he said shyly.

'You know where I work and what I do for a living, that's almost more than I know about you.' She put her cup down carefully in its saucer. 'I would like to know a lot more.'

'Ask away, I'll try to answer the best I can, but don't get too personal!'

Where to start? she thought. 'I know your name is Ben and where you work, but that's about all, so tell me – where do you live, how big is your family, where did you go to school, is this your first job…?'

'Hold on, one question at a time!' Ben pleaded, shaking his head as if to clear it.

Sophie smiled again. 'Ok, I'll try to be a little less eager with my questions, so start off by telling me about your family.'

'I live with my aunt and uncle. He has a greengrocer's, which is what got me interested in food and cooking. It's another hard job with long hours but not as many hours as a chef. We live in a nice house in Hammersmith, which is great for me as I can cycle to the hotel – as long as I can avoid getting knocked down by some stupid motorist!' Sophie watched his face as he spoke. It was an excitable, emotional face, especially when he spoke of his aunt and uncle.

'What about your parents?' she asked.

'That's possibly for another day and another time.' The way he spoke warned Sophie not to take it any further. 'Now what about you?' Ben leant forward, their hands almost touching.

'Well, I live with my dad not a million miles from you, but not in such a grand area. We have a two-bedroom flat in Auriol House – that's in Ellerslie Road. I don't suppose you know White City, do you?' Ben tried to remember if he had ever ventured there and thought he must have travelled through it on his way somewhere, but for the life of him he couldn't really remember.

'Sorry, I know of it, but you're right, I haven't been there.'

Sophie told Ben some more about her life. 'My dad works in the Hammersmith Hospital. He's a porter in the very posh part which is mainly for private patients. Like us it can be long hours for not very much in return. The good thing about it is that he can get there easily as it's only a couple of miles from the flat, and the bus service is reasonable.'

There was a pause as they both took in each other's brief family story.

'What about your mum?' As soon as it was out of his mouth Ben regretted asking the question. He knew that if Sophie had wanted to tell him about her mum she would have.

Sophie looked down into her empty cup. 'Like you said, Ben, perhaps that's for another time.'

Ben liked sitting with Sophie, he liked it a lot, but he knew that they had long working hours ahead of them and he could already feel his eyelids drooping. Sophie realised they were both tired, and anyway it looked as if the café owner was starting to clear everything away.

'I think he's trying to tell us something, don't you?'

Ben nodded his head in agreement. 'I've really enjoyed having coffee with you,' he blurted out. He was embarrassed, shy, and lost for words.

Sophie looked up and smiled. 'Perhaps we can do it again?'

Ben was rushing. 'Tomorrow,' he asked, 'what about tomorrow?'

Sophie could see a look of something akin to panic on his face and laughed. 'Tomorrow, then. I'll be here perhaps a little earlier.'

'I'll have to get my bike, its back at the hotel.'

As they left the café Sophie linked her arm with his. 'I'll walk back with you, it's on the way to the tube.'

When they reached the hotel, Ben gulped. What should he do? Kiss her? Shake her hand? Wave? He got on his bike and before he knew what was happening, she reached up and kissed him lightly on the cheek.

'See you tomorrow,' she said.

The following day Rodger watched his friend burst through the doors of the kitchen. 'Calm down, you're not late, there's still a couple of minutes to go before the boss sacks you.'

'Ha ha, very funny.'

Ben straightened his whites and went to his workstation. He waited for the instructions to come as to what was needed. He had been making pastry for a couple of days and was getting quite good at it, but he knew that he would have many more hours mixing, kneading, piping and shaping before he got to a standard that was good enough for his boss. He told Rodger he was meeting Sophie again, to which Rodger made some very crude gestures and sounds like a bull in the mating season. They both had a good laugh and Rodger told Ben he was a lucky bastard.

The following afternoon Sophie turned up at the café a little earlier as promised, and was waiting for him. He came in looking nervously round until he saw her, then seemed to calm a little until he opened his mouth and nothing came out. Why he felt so embarrassed, he couldn't figure out. It was the girl, she must have something special about her, her personality perhaps, or was it that he just fancied her like hell? He went to the counter and ordered a cappuccino.

'Am I late?' he asked.

'No, it's me, I'm rather early. I finished before time and managed to get away without being called back for any stupid mistakes made by any of the others.'

They sat and talked about members of staff – those they liked, those they didn't. Sophie was spending part of her day in the hotel's office and on reception. It was what she really wanted to do and her enthusiasm was palpable.

'Is that what you see yourself doing in a couple of years?'

'Oh yes.' Sophie's eyes glinted. 'I don't want to be a full-time waitress or even a part-time waitress for ever.'

Ben could tell that this was someone who knew exactly where she was going and how she was going to get there. He felt that their aims seemed to be very similar, and if Sophie was going to achieve her goal it would mean hard work and long hours just the same as for him.

Sophie went on, 'I would like to be on the management team of a large hotel, somewhere that made the job worthwhile and where I could achieve my dreams. I know you want to get on too, so what's *your* plan?'

Ben toyed with his cup and spoon. 'I want to be a good chef and run my own kitchen … but if I'm really honest, what I really want is to own my own restaurant and cook exciting food I think customers would like.'

'Will that take a great deal of time and training?'

Ben looked at her with an eager expression on his face. 'It will take perseverance, stubbornness, determination, and sheer bloody mindedness, and I think I have those by the bucket load!'

Sophie checked her watch. 'I have to go and get a few things for home and my dad will expect me to have his dinner ready when he gets in.'

'No peace for the wicked, then – but I'm sure you're not wicked,' Ben said softly.

Sophie smiled. 'Don't you believe it! Beneath this tender and gentle façade there lies a woman of steel.'

They looked at each other for a moment without speaking.

Ben said, 'Shall we do the same tomorrow?'

'As long as our shifts allow,' Sophie said with the coy smile that Ben liked so much.

They left the café and followed the same pattern as the previous day, walking back so that Ben could collect his bike, and Sophie gave him a gentle peck on the cheek before she headed towards the tube.

6

Their meetings became more and more difficult to organise, as shift patterns, college, and family pressure resulted in Ben and Sophie only being able to meet once a week. They had tried to see a film, *Doctor Zhivago*, but soon discovered that their life-styles made it virtually impossible to sit through a film of that length. Their heads were soon on each other's shoulders as their eyes closed. They slept through most of the film only to be woken by an usherette when all the other film-goers had left the cinema. Sophie had asked Ben to her place for a meal when they next planned to meet, and to prevent any arguments about who cooked she suggested fish and chips from the local chippy which was, in her opinion, one of the best. Ben took her up on her offer and they decided to get together on their next available date.

Sophie said anxiously, 'Don't expect too much, it's just me and dad in a two-bed council flat.'

Ben smiled at her. 'I don't care if it's a rabbit hutch if we can get some time together. Will your dad be there?'

'Yes, but he doesn't bite.'

Ben felt a little nervous at the prospect and his initial reaction was to suggest a different time when her father would be out, but he thought in the end it would be better to get a meeting with her dad over with.

'What's he like, your dad?'

'Well, to me he's the gentlest of people. He can be very quiet and sometimes you may think he's ignoring you, but he is listening to every word. Sadly, since my mum died, he has become less of the person I used to know.'

To Ben it sounded similar to how his mum was when his dad died. *This is going to be difficult*, he thought, but he wanted to get to know Sophie's dad if he could.

On the Friday of the following week Ben and Sophie met after their shifts, Ben travelling in by tube so he didn't have to worry about his bike. Sophie grabbed his hand. 'Come on,' she said as she led him towards the tube station.

The block that Sophie lived in was four storeys high with balconies to the first, second, and third floors. They were built of red brick with white picking out the bottom of the balconies and the windows in the stairwell. The roof looked as if it had a metal barrier going around its full length and he wondered if that was there to prevent jumpers. As they walked up the stairs, Ben could hear their footsteps echo. It seemed to be an ok place to live, but Ben liked his uncle and aunt's house better.

They reached Sophie's door. 'Here we are,' and she took her key out of her purse and let them into a small hallway. The flat was spotless and everything was in its place. Ben looked around and noticed two pictures on the wall, one of the 'Green Lady' which he had seen many times before, and another of a landscape which couldn't be further from London if it tried.

'My dad's not home yet so make yourself at home. I'll wait until he comes in and then we can go to the chippy.'

The front room was comfortable and felt welcoming. Ben sat on the sofa knowing that fathers normally sat in an armchair and woe betide anyone who took their seat. It was only ten minutes or so before there was the sound of a key turning in the front door lock. Ben stood up ready to greet Sophie's dad.

'Dad this is Ben, Ben this is my dad.' Sophie smiled nervously. Ben looked at the man shaking his hand; not that tall but fairly well built, his smile showing a resemblance to Sophie that was unmistakeable. He could see so many features that he had passed on to her.

'Pleased to meet you.' Ben hesitated. *Do I call him 'Sir'?* He didn't know, so just left it at that.

'Good to meet you, Ben. Sophie has told me a lot about you.'

'I hope nothing too bad,' Ben replied, smiling.

Sophie's father had a London accent. Whether it was 'cockney' or not he couldn't say, but it was definitely London.

'Dad, we're going to the chippy, what would you like?'

Her dad took his jacket off and stretched his shoulders. 'Rock salmon and chips, please, and if you hang on I'll get you some money.'

'It's ok, dad, I've got enough.'

She grabbed Ben's hand and led him towards the door. When they were outside Ben asked her, 'What should I call your dad?'

'Well, his name is Derek, so why not call him that?'

That didn't help Ben much, but he would see if he could sort things out when they got back to the flat. It didn't take long to get the fish and chips. Sophie had the same as her dad and Ben had cod. The smell of the chippy made them both salivate and Ben could hear his stomach rumble. Back at the flat, Sophie's dad had set the table in the kitchen. It was just big enough to get three round it. Vinegar and salt were placed in the centre on a gingham tablecloth of red and white squares.

'Do you want something to drink?' Sophie's dad asked Ben. 'I've got a couple of tins of light ale if you fancy it.'

'Thanks, that will do nicely.'

Sophie said, 'I'll just have a glass of water.'

They sat down to their meal and it was Sophie who started the conversation. 'Dad, Ben asked me what he should call you?'

Ben blushed as Sophie's dad looked him squarely in the face. 'Um... perhaps he could call me by my name, what do you think?' he said with a twinkle in his eye.

Ben grinned. 'Derek?'

'That's right.'

The evening flew by, the conversation centring mostly on the hotel and the people who worked there. Ben politely asked Sophie's dad about his work, but Derek seemed reticent about what his duties were. He left the flat at eleven o'clock. He had to get home, get some sleep and be ready for another working day even though it was a Saturday. It was then he remembered he was going to assist Burdett with the catering at Steyning's place. He got to the hotel early and was waiting for Burdett when he arrived.

'Good to see you're early, Ben. Come on, we've got a lot to do.' Ben followed Burdett into the kitchen.

'We take only what we need and no more. We have the run of his kitchen and he has ample utensils for preparation and presentation.'

They took their time, Burdett making sure that everything was in order. The produce was gathered together and placed into cool bags where needed. Burdett had an estate car which made everything a lot easier to arrange. They set off and within minutes they were outside Steyning's house. As they made their way up the steps to the front door, Burdett turned to Ben and chuckled. 'Better take your shoes off or you'll incur the wrath of the wicked witch of the north.'

He wasn't wrong. She opened the door and looked at them as if they had just crawled out of a cess pit. 'You know where the kitchen is so get on with it and don't make a mess.'

They carried their produce and dishes through the hall to the kitchen. Ben was impressed by its layout and modern lines.

'What time is the meal to be ready for?'

'Not till nine o'clock, so we have plenty of time.'

They worked through the day preparing everything meticulously. As Burdett kept on impressing on him, this was a very expensive meal and everything had to be perfect. 'If we make a good job of this and create a good impression, more of the same is likely to follow.'

Towards the end of the afternoon Steyning came into the kitchen to see how things were going. He had a good look at all the components of the meal and seemed satisfied. He asked Burdett if there would be plenty for six, to which Burdett replied without hesitation that there would be more than ample. Steyning left them to get on with their work.

As the day went on and the preparation was nearing completion, Ben asked if Burdett had ever had a good look around the house. He replied that he had and that it was opulent to the extent that his wages would not even buy a toilet roll in this house. He suggested to Ben that if he was careful he could go and have a nose round as long as he didn't bump into the wicked witch.

'I'll avoid her like the plague!'

'Be quick, then.'

With that, Ben headed out of the kitchen and into the main part of the house. Opulent wasn't the word, simply magnificent summed it up better. Ben tiptoed up the curving staircase and as he did, he heard Steyning singing – *out of tune* he thought, and he appeared not to know the words of the song he was trying to sing. Ben could see Steyning through the open door of his bedroom. His curiosity getting the better of him, he stood and watched Steyning as he hung up a suit up and straightened it. To his surprise, he saw Steyning pick up a small sachet of something and place it in the pocket of his suit jacket. He patted the pocket and with a satisfied smile said aloud, 'Later, later.' Ben turned and quietly made his way back to the kitchen.

When Ben reached the kitchen, he suddenly thought about the evening ahead and asked Burdett who would be serving table? Burdett told him it wouldn't be them and that one of Steyning's guests would bring a sort of valet or manservant with him and he would wait on table. Steyning had made it perfectly clear to Burdett that neither he nor Ben should go anywhere near the dining room.

'Is it that hush hush?' asked Ben

'Believe me, I wouldn't go within a mile of the dining room when they get started.'

The remainder of their time was taken with the cooking and presentation of the meal. As Burdett had told Ben, everything had to be 'just so' and there would be no room for error. At eight o'clock a very smartly dressed individual appeared at the kitchen door. He was at least six foot tall, and although not the most powerfully built man Ben had ever seen, he looked as if he could control most situations whether mental or physical. He did not offer his name, but made it very clear, in quiet and rather menacing tones, that he would collect the dishes when they were ready and return them when finished. His appearance was very close to that of the GIs Ben had seen on the TV when footage from Vietnam was on the news. His close-cropped hair, clean lines and upright carriage, gave him a military air. Both Burdett and Ben had no problem with his instructions and had no intention of suggesting anything different; they agreed there was something a little intimidating about the man.

At eight-thirty Ben heard the doorbell ring and he thought he could hear Steyning welcoming various guests. The meal started at nine and went according to plan. What happened behind the dining room door would remain a mystery to them.

*

In the dining room, six men sat around an elegant Louis XIV dining table. At the head was an American, and at the foot of the table sat Steyning with another two on either side. All the men were well attired in suits of very expensive cut.

The American began. 'We have a great deal to discuss and I hope you have all prepared well.' His voice was clearly used to giving orders and the expression on the faces of the others was accepting of this. Introductions were made. Names were given, and nationalities - clearly, they were not all acquainted. The first was an Italian, Aldo, who sat with an air of supreme self-assurance that seemed to be shared by all of those present. The second, François, was from Paris, and sitting across the table was Christoph from the Netherlands. The last, which came as a surprise to Steyning, was another Englishman whom he had not met before although he had a vague recollection of him; this was Joseph, whose Brummie accent was unmistakeable.

Steyning introduced himself. 'I'm Max, your host for the evening. If you need anything, please ask.'

The American then began, 'Although we don't all know each other, you all know me. I am Adam. Now let's get started.'

The meeting in the dining room covered the many aspects of their business. The prepared agenda was strictly followed and each item was given only a certain amount of time. If it appeared they were running on too long, Adam stepped in and moved the discussion on. It was stressed that profits had not been as high as anticipated and individual explanations were given by each person with the exception of Joseph, who remained tight-lipped, listening intently.

*

As the dishes were served, Ben set to work washing and cleaning as Burdett finished off the courses. After the final plate had been carried away by the un-named man, Burdett gave Ben a hand and between them they completed the clearing up. As they came to the end of their tasks, both Burdett and Ben sighed with relief; it had been hard work, but hopefully it would be well remunerated.

The so-called waiter or bodyguard soon appeared with two envelopes, which he gave to Burdett. 'These are from Mr Steyning. He and his guests have asked me to pass on their appreciation for all you have done this evening.'

Burdett took the envelopes and nodded to him. 'Thank you. We'll be on our way now. Come on, Ben, let's go.' They collected their possessions and coats and headed out of the kitchen. Ben noticed how the waiter/bodyguard followed them closely until they reached the front door.

Burdett turned. 'Goodnight,' he said to the figure in the doorway. The man just held up his hand in acknowledgement and was gone.

7

In the dining room it took the members of the meeting well into the night to make sure everything was covered, and even then, Adam looked at Steyning and said that another gathering would be necessary not only to continue with the current discussions but also to prepare the ground for the launch of a new product which it would be in everybody's interest to learn in detail.

'I can't tell you much at the moment, but it is something that the boys in the lab have been developing for some time. It will entail a process that will circumnavigate the necessity to grow the raw material.' He glanced again at Steyning. 'I suggest that we re-convene here in six weeks' time. I know you have other pressing engagements, but this is something that we need to get out to suppliers as quickly as possible.' Steyning knew it was not a request; it was a command.

They all checked their diaries and agreed the date. The man known as Adam stood up. 'Well, gentlemen, this has been a very productive meeting and I look forward to seeing you all in six weeks.' That was his way of closing the meeting and telling those present to leave. The men got to their feet and said their farewells.

Just before he departed, Adam paused and opened his briefcase, removing a small sachet. He turned to look at Steyning. 'Thanks for tonight, it went well.' He held out his hand and Steyning took the proffered sachet.

Adam frowned as he handed it over. 'You look a little confused, Max, is there anything troubling you?'

'I can't quite figure out where Joseph fits into the business. He didn't have much to say.'

Adam's attitude was relaxed and he seemed perfectly at ease with the question. 'Joseph is a chemical engineer and a very good one. He is what you could call my technical adviser. He's been in America helping to prepare the new product for its launch, and now he is helping us to prepare the way for a new stage in our business plan. I hope that sets your mind at rest.'

Steyning felt a wave of relief flood over him. 'Thanks for that, Adam.'

Adam made his way to the door, which was being held open by his man Friday. Cars had already ferried away the other diners as dawn was breaking.

*

As Burdett and Ben got into the car, Burdett said it had been a bit tricky in places but apparently Steyning had been satisfied. Burdett opened one of the envelopes; it contained the invoice he had given Steyning at the start of the evening, which Steyning was paying in cash. Burdett whistled. It had not been a cheap meal. He leafed through the five hundred pounds with a satisfied look. The second envelope was a surprise as all that was written inside was 'thanks'. It contained a further one hundred pounds. Burdett looked across at Ben. 'Well, you've earned quite a bit tonight.' He handed over forty pounds to Ben, who couldn't believe his luck.

'What's this?' he asked.

'It's what you call a very nice tip, so don't question it, just enjoy spending it.'

The following day Ben arrived at work and got on with his

tasks for the day. Burdett was called to the manager's office and returned with a smile on his face. He clapped Ben on the back.

'Well, we must have done a good job – we've been asked to supply another one in six weeks' time.'

Ben was more than happy. He could almost feel the money in his pocket. A few more of these and he would be able to take Sophie out for several slap-up meals – provided they could keep awake! He would be able to tell her when they next met, hopefully the following Tuesday. In the meantime, life continued to be hard graft and long hours; but he knew his day would come.

Ben and Sophie's relationship continued to grow, and they became known as a 'couple' by the staff in the hotel. They were both proving good in their respective roles and it looked as if their futures were becoming secure. Ben thought it was time he took Sophie to his home and showed her where he lived, so when they next met he suggested that he return the favour and that she could have fish and chips at his house. Sophie looked keen, but wanted to check with her dad.

She was very nervous when the day arrived. Ben had arranged to call for her and when he picked her up he just couldn't believe how lucky he was. He looked at her with wide eyes; she was wonderful. She was wearing a maxi-length coat in black with pink bands across the shoulders and another around the waist. Her hair gleamed soft and shiny. He looked at her face – it looked so beautiful he wanted to kiss her, but she brought him down to earth as she said 'see you later' to her father. As she walked towards him, he could see that beneath the coat she was wearing a pink mini dress which showed off her legs to their best advantage, and on her feet were pink suede shoes with straps and buckles; nothing showy, just right. This was the girl who was going out with him! He still couldn't believe it and gulped in a lungful of air, thinking *Lucky isn't the word!*

Ben's uncle and aunt had made a special point of being at home, which was not exactly what Ben had planned. They were eager to meet this 'Sophie' that Ben talked about so much. He had tried to explain to Sophie that they would be at home when she arrived, but would be going out after they had had a chance to meet her. His uncle had promised to take his aunt to see a film, so hopefully they would have some time to themselves. This didn't help Sophie's nerves, which grew worse when Ben said, 'Here we are.'

She looked at the smart Edwardian end-of-terrace house with steps leading up to a black door with shiny brass fittings. Sophie thought that if this was the outside, what was waiting for her inside?

'This is your house?' Sophie asked with some disbelief.

'Yes – well, it's my uncle's. Do you like it?'

'It's lovely.' She gripped Ben's hand tightly as they walked up the steps. He opened the door and led her into the hall where she was even more impressed with the beautiful staircase leading to the first floor. *So posh*, she thought. Ben guided her into the living room where his uncle was sitting in his favourite chair, reading the paper. He jumped up as they entered and regarded Sophie.

'So, you're the young lady Ben has been telling us about.'

Sophie was a little embarrassed but held out her hand, which surprised Ben's uncle. He gently shook her hand and was surprised again as he did not expect such a firm handshake. She was proving to be an unexpectedly delightful young girl who had, besides, a smile that would have men fighting for it.

'And this is my wife Sarah, who you can guess is Ben's aunt.'

'Let me take your coat.' Sarah took Sophie's coat and carefully hung it on the coat rack. She then herded them into the sitting room. As she entered, Sophie's gaze took in the room. It was furnished with a large three-seater sofa and two armchairs that looked decidedly classy. The TV in one corner looked state of the art and Sophie thought that though the paintings on the walls were possibly not to her taste, they were on a par with the rest of the décor.

'Would anyone like a drink? What about you, Sophie?'

'Have you any lemonade?'

Sophie sat down on the sofa next to Ben. 'You have a lovely home,' she said to Ben's aunt with a certain amount of envy.

'It's taken a long time to get it just the way we want it, but it's been worth it.'

The conversation centred on the house and life at the hotel. Ben's aunt asked Sophie what she hoped to do in the future which gave Sophie the opportunity to relax and speak more freely. After they had finished their drinks, Steven stood and, looking at his wife, said they didn't want to be late for the start of the film and that they had better be making a move. Sarah stood too, and smiling at Sophie, said she hoped this would be the first of many meetings. Sophie returned her smile saying she hoped so too.

As soon as the front door closed, both Ben and Sophie sighed with a certain amount of relief. Ben took Sophie by the shoulders and kissed her gently on the lips.

'What I would really like to do now,' Sophie said, 'is absolutely nothing. Can we just stay in? Every time we meet we seem to be either dashing to work or back to our homes. I really would love to just relax.'

Could Ben sacrifice a fish and chip supper to spend an evening alone this lovely thing? He definitely could, and would.

'I think the TV and beans on toast. What do you say?'

'That would be my kind of evening,' she grinned.

Ben went into the kitchen to sort out the bits and pieces needed for their snacky meal.

'Can I use your toilet, Ben?'

'It's upstairs, first on the left.' Sophie climbed the stairs, noticing the smooth polished banister rail and the pattern of the carpet. *Nice*, she thought.

She opened the bathroom door and was surprised again. It was a large room with a bath, toilet, sink, and what she didn't expect – a shower. She had only experienced showers at the swimming pool. She looked at the way the door to the cubicle closed and how the base had a shiny drain, and it was so good! How quick it would be to shower instead of filling a bath. She thought of asking if she could have a shower, but then thought better of it; it might give Ben ideas.

When she returned to the sitting room, she just had to mention the shower. Ben's reaction was an amused one.

'My uncle is a great follower of innovation, and especially 'Tomorrow's World'. They had shown a presentation on the 'home of the future' and Uncle Steven just had to get a shower installed!'

It was one of the first electric showers on the market and was worth every penny. Both Ben and his uncle used the shower daily. It saved time and water. Ben was able to get up, shower and get fully dressed in half the time it took to sort out a bath, and he didn't have to go 'dirty' several days a week like most people who only took a bath on Sundays. Ben could see the look of envy on Sophie's face and he thought he would show off some of the other things his uncle had invested in.

'Come and have a look at these other gadgets,'

He took her hand and led her into the kitchen. She couldn't believe her eyes. Everything was built in. There were cupboards below a marble work surface and above, and the cooker had more knobs on it than she had ever seen before. So much room!

'Wow,' was all that she could say as she compared it with her own tiny kitchen, every item taking up room and a table stuck in the middle. She walked around touching surfaces, opening cupboards, and pulling out drawers. When Ben thought she had seen enough he took her by the hand and led her back to the sitting room.

'You sit there and I'll call you when the food's ready.'

She looked at him still with a look of amazement on her face. But she couldn't sit still; she got up and walked around, touching side-tables, lamps, and cushions. She walked into the kitchen, admiring it yet again. As she glanced out of the window she stopped suddenly, her hand to her mouth. 'You've got a garden!' The words almost jumped out of her mouth.

'Yes, it's not very big, but I like it.'

'Not very big!' she spluttered. 'Can I see it, Ben, please?'

'It's a bit dark to have a good look.'

'I don't care, please let me see.' Ben unlocked the door to the garden and switched on an outside light. The garden suddenly came alive as the light flowed over the lawn and flower beds.

Sophie clutched at Ben's arm. 'Can I?' she said, almost choking with excitement.

'Sure, help yourself, but don't be too long or your beans will get cold.'

Sophie stepped onto a paved patio area and almost ran to the nearest flower bed trying to take everything in. She could see that the garden wasn't massive, but it was big enough, to her mind. The lawn was bordered on one side by a narrow drive that ran alongside the house and led to a garage. The path on the other side led to a small fenced gravelled area which sported a bird bath in the centre. It was just amazing to Sophie, who had always dreamed of having a garden, and immediately she made a promise to herself that one day she would have one just like this.

'The food's ready,' Ben called.

'Oh, do I have to come in?'

'Yes, you do, now hurry up!'

Slowly Sophie dragged herself back indoors and Ben turned off the outside light. They decided to eat in the kitchen and sat down to their feast of beans on toast. Ben had been just a little creative by putting some grated cheese on the top of Sophie's and a fried egg on top of his. They sat and chatted, mainly about the garden. Sophie just kept on with questions – how big was it, what plants grew in which bed, who looked after it, did Ben do anything. Ben had never seen her so excited and explained as best he could that his aunt was the real gardener and was the one who loved her flowers. Ben's job was cutting the grass and keeping things tidy whilst his uncle did any heavy-duty stuff. Although his uncle was a greengrocer, Ben went on, he still enjoyed growing some salad veg such as lettuce and tomatoes, radishes and so on. Ben's aunt also had a liking for herbs.

'One day I'll show you the garden in daylight and then you can fully appreciate it,' he told Sophie. They finished their meal and cleared away the plates.

'Come on, let's go and sit down,' he said. They returned to the sitting room and Ben opened up the radiogram. 'Any music you fancy? We have quite a collection. My uncle is a great Dusty Springfield fan and my aunt, believe it or not, likes some opera.'

'Dusty would be good.' Sophie lay back and let out a sigh of contentment.

As Dusty's voice started to fill the room, Ben joined Sophie on the sofa.

'I've had a lovely evening, Ben. 'You have a lovely home and a wonderful garden.' Sophie put a lot of emphasis on the word garden.

Ben put his arm around her. 'I thought you looked a little down when I picked you up tonight. Is anything wrong?'

Sophie's eyes filled with tears. 'It's the anniversary of my mum's death. Sorry – it's always something that still affects me no matter what I'm doing.'

'Do you want to talk about it?' Ben asked, not knowing what sort of reaction he would get.

Sophie's shoulders drooped. 'It's not a very nice story. I don't usually talk about it, only to my dad, and that's when he wants to talk, which isn't often.'

Ben could see that Sophie was struggling to decide if she would tell him about her mother or not.

'If I tell you *my* story, will you tell me yours?'

It was not what Ben was expecting, but maybe it would do him good to tell Sophie about Jack, and his mum and dad too. 'Ok, it's a deal.'

8

Sophie looked around the room as if she was plucking up the courage to start. She told Ben how her mum and dad met and that her mum had fallen pregnant with her when she was only seventeen. Her dad was only two years older, so really they were both still kids. They got married and lived with her mum's parents. They had a stroke of luck when a council flat came up for rent, and with the help of relations who worked for the council, they managed to secure it. Sophie shifted nervously on the sofa.

'Time went by and Mum began to feel she had lost her youth and that there was no excitement in her life. She became depressed and had difficulty in getting a good night's sleep. My dad tried to take her to the doctor's but she resisted.' Sophie had trouble continuing; she became choked with emotion and Ben gently placed his arm around her shoulders.

'Apparently, after several attempts, my dad managed to get my mum to the surgery. I don't know the ins and outs of what went on, but my dad said she was prescribed Valium, which was supposed to help her sleep. Not very long after her first prescription was filled, she met a woman about the same age waiting at the chemist's for the same drug. They struck up a friendship and would meet in each other's flats when the husbands were at work and the kids at school. The story goes that this new friend encouraged my mum to take stronger and stronger pills and potions, starting with the Valium then going on to amphetamines, which led to more serious stuff.

'My dad reckons they were both trying to get some of their youth back. They could be seen out doing some crazy things – not harming anyone, just annoying people. My mum's friend – I think her name was Carol – tried to get my mum to go to parties with her. I think my mum may have gone to one or two but she never spoke about them. Carol had told her that to get what she wanted it would be easy as long as she kept certain American gentlemen happy. My mum was good-looking, but vulnerable, which Carol took advantage of. It got to a stage where my dad started noticing housekeeping money vanishing very quickly and things disappearing from the flat. My dad had worked hard and saved a little money but that was vanishing fast too. We don't know how my mother got into hard drugs. It's thought that it was just a progression and her trying to get a better feeling about herself. Anyway, it all ended when I got home from school and found both of them lying on the floor of the sitting room. Mum's friend was breathing but my mum didn't show any signs of life. I ran to the nearest phone box and dialled 999.'

Ben could feel Sophie start to tremble and he didn't know if she would be able to continue. He asked her if she wanted to stop, but she told him she needed to tell him everything. She wiped her eyes and started again. When the ambulance and police arrived, things were bad. I had stayed in the flat. I was scared and felt sick. I tried to get my mum to sit up and talk but she just fell back and I couldn't hold her. Noises were coming from her friend, so I tried to get her to talk too, but could only get groans and her being sick.

I could see the police speaking very quietly to the ambulance men and I saw them shake their heads. Then they knocked on our neighbour's door and asked them to look after me. They were ok, but not exactly friends of the family due to my mother creating hell with them, but they said I could stay with them until my dad could be reached. As I went into my neighbour's flat I could see the ambulance men struggling to put my mum's friend into a wheelchair. Mum was still lying on the floor. A few minutes later I heard my dad's voice asking where I was. The next thing he was hammering on the door. As soon as he saw me he grabbed me and hugged me tight. I could feel him shaking. I asked what was happening and all he could say was that mum had had a terrible accident. My dad asked the neighbours if they would look after me until he could get things sorted out, and left me with them.

It took nearly four hours before he came to get me. He took me to our flat and I could see that he had tried to clean the area where Mum had been lying. When I asked what was happening, he took my hand and told me that mum had died. He did it as gently as possible. I was only twelve.

Sophie's dad had arranged for her mother to be cremated. A small service was held in the chapel of the crematorium with just her and her dad and the two neighbours.

'I remember being distraught to think that this was all the send-off Mum would get. She was worth more than that. I held onto Dad's hand tightly and I saw tears appear in his eyes and I knew he really loved her.'

Sophie continued, 'After the funeral, me and my dad sat for a long time just wondering what we were going to do. I couldn't think any higher of my dad. He coped with the death of his wife, he kept his job, and he looked after me. We both worked together

- 57 -

and fell into a pretty good routine. I helped with the cleaning and washing and did a bit of shopping. My dad went to work and also did the rest of the housework and the main shop. He doesn't speak about it now. I think he just wants the past to be the past and not interfere with the future. So now we are a good team and look after each other.'

She looked into Ben's eyes and he could see that she had held back her tears.

'What about you, you've got to tell me your story now.'

Ben took a deep breath. 'Do you really want me to tell you? Haven't you had enough for one night?'

'No, Ben, I need someone to understand what I have been through and I need to know I am not the only one who has felt pain like this.'

For Ben it was not easy, but he had promised, and like Jack had told him, always fulfil your promises. Ben started by trying to explain to Sophie just how much Jack meant to him. He was not only his big brother but he was Ben's hero. The way Jack led his life seemed to be full of so much excitement, so much fun, so much life, the places he went to, the people he talked about – Ben told her how he just listened wide-eyed to his stories.

He then started telling Sophie what had happened, how he was five years younger than Jack who was their mum's blue-eyed boy and could do no wrong; how after their father died, Jack and uncle Steven took great care of their mum, but she retreated into herself although in time they thought they had brought her back to her previous self. Jack had told him of the clubs he visited and how he would dance to the latest music from the UK and the States. He told him of the girls he met and how he fell in love with most of them. What he didn't tell him, Ben said, was how he managed to keep going to the early hours of the morning and still go to work but he could see that some days he seemed to be in another world and it became hard to get him to concentrate. Then came the terrible news that Jack had been found dead outside one of the clubs. 'My mother couldn't cope with losing first my dad and now Jack. It was all too much.'

Ben described how his mother deteriorated and finally passed away after catching pneumonia. They both fell silent for a while, thinking about those they had lost. Ben felt anger build inside him as he thought of how Jack had met his death. He still believed that Jack would not have taken dangerous pills; he was just certain. He remembered his promise to Jack's memory to find out who was responsible for his death, and he was determined to keep it.

As they sat quietly their heads met, and slowly their eyes closed. It had taken a great deal out of both of them to tell their stories. The key turning in the front door woke them up with a start. Ben's aunt and uncle appeared in the doorway and surveyed the scene. Both Ben and Sophie rubbed their eyes and looked as if they had been doing nothing but sleeping.

Ben leaped to his feet. 'Did you like the film?' He had no idea what they had watched.

His aunt looked scornfully at her husband. 'Can you believe it, he took me to see a cowboy film. I ask you!'

Ben and Sophie couldn't help smiling.

Sophie asked, 'What film did you see?'

'Actually, it turned out to be quite good,' she laughed.

Ben's uncle then stepped into the conversation. 'It was great. It had comedy and tragedy and fantastic songs and music.'

'Yes, but what was it called?' Ben asked impatiently.

''Butch Cassidy and the Sundance Kid', his aunt told him, and started to sing 'Raindrops keep falling on my head'. She took off her coat and headed for the kitchen, still singing. 'Who's for coffee?'

'Yes, please,' both replied.

'What about you, Butch Cassidy?' she called out to her husband with a giggle.

'Yes, please.' Then to everyone's exasperation he too began to sing, not very melodiously.

As Ben sat there with his coffee he felt good, that with their shared conversation he and Sophie had created a bond that would hopefully last a lifetime. And he could still look forward to showing her the garden in the daylight.

Steven offered to run Sophie home as it was getting late and it wasn't far. Sophie looked at Ben, who said he would come along to keep her company, and they both smiled. Ben's aunt and uncle cleared the cups away and Sophie told them how much she had liked their garden.

'Have another look. I'm sure we've got a few minutes to spare,' said Steven. He opened the kitchen door and turned on the light. Sophie looked at Ben and took his hand, leading him out into the garden.

'Ben, can I ask you for a big favour?'

'Sure, anything.'

'It's about something I found that belonged to my mum.' Ben's curiosity was aroused and he asked what it was.

'I found an old biscuit tin in the back of one of our cupboards. It was where my mum kept her 'stuff'.'

'What sort of stuff?'

'Stuff to do with the drugs she'd been taking. I opened it up and saw there were syringes and things that I didn't understand and also some little bags of powder. I can't bring myself to handle anything that my mum had used to kill herself with. I quickly closed the tin and put it back where I found it. 'Could you get rid of it for me?'

It was not a request that Ben had come across before, but he could see no problem in getting rid of something like that. 'If you give it to me when we take you home, I'll dispose of it for you.'

Sophie gripped his hand. 'Thanks, Ben.'

She turned her attention back to the garden that she had fallen in love with. She could almost dance she felt so happy, and with Ben's aunt singing about raindrops life just seemed so good.

They reached Sophie's flat very quickly. Ben got out of the car and told his uncle he would walk Sophie to her front door.

'I won't be long.'

'Take your time, I'm not going anywhere.'

As they reached the door she turned to Ben. 'What a wonderful evening. I feel good that we spoke, Ben, it feels as if a weight has been lifted from my shoulders.'

He turned her towards him and kissed her gently. She didn't resist and they merged into one another's embrace.

Sophie eased back from him. 'Will you still help get rid of my mum's stuff?' she asked.

'Go and get it. I won't come in, in case I wake your father.'

'Won't be a sec,' she said as she disappeared into the flat. She returned very quickly, clutching a shortbread biscuit tin with a picture of the Scottish Highlands on the lid. She held it out towards Ben. 'This is what I told you about. I just want it out of the flat and not see it ever again.'

Ben took the tin. It was light, but he could hear something loose inside. He would check it out when he got home as he didn't want to ask any questions about its contents.

Sophie stepped forward and kissed him again. 'Ben, you're very lucky to have your nice home and lovely aunt and uncle.'

'I suppose I am, but I think I would rather have my mum, dad, and brother with me than anyone else.'

Ben could see that for once he had someone close who understood how he felt, and in return, he could see how Sophie's life had been turned upside down by the events she had related. Ben made his way along the passageway leading from her flat. He turned and waved and she blew him a kiss. Back at the car, Steven noticed that Ben was carrying a tin of some description.

'Has she given you a box of biscuits?' he asked.

'No, it's some bits and pieces of her mum's that she has asked me to get rid of. She didn't have the heart to do it herself.' Ben thought that was as near to the truth as he wanted to get.

When they got back to the house, his aunt and uncle agreed that Sophie was a lovely girl and they both hoped it would turn into a long term-relationship, but understood how things had a habit of turning out not as one expected or would have liked. Ben said his goodnights and went to his room.

He closed the door and sat on his bed. He looked at the tin Sophie had given him and opened it cautiously. What he saw made him wince. It contained two syringes, a thick rubber band, silver paper, a spoon, and two small sachets of white powder. He had never been involved with drugs before and could not imagine what some of the items were used for. He looked carefully at the sachets of powder and wondered if they were the reason for Sophie's mum's death. He made a mental note to ask Sophie if she knew, and realised he would have to tread very carefully.

During his break the following day, Ben sought Sophie out. She was pleased to see him and her eyes shone when they kissed quickly. 'Have you been able to get rid of that awful tin?'

'Almost, but I have to be careful. I don't want it to get into anywhere it may cause harm.'

Sophie nodded.

'Tell me, is the stuff in the small packets the cause of your mum's death?' His voice was tender and caring.

Sophie gulped, but nodded her head. 'Yes, the police told my dad that it was a concoction of heroin and cocaine called a 'speedball' and that it was pretty lethal. They took away two sachets but I found those other two and put them into the tin.'

Ben changed the subject quickly. 'I told my aunt how much you liked the garden and she wants you to go over to her house so she can show it to you in its full glory. The good thing is, I don't need to be with you, so you can go on one of your days off.' He observed the look of excitement on Sophie's face, but for the life of him he couldn't understand how people could get so excited over a garden.

'That would be lovely. Could you tell her I'm off next Thursday and if it's ok with her I could be at your house by, say, ten o'clock.'

'Make it eleven. My aunt's normally busy getting my uncle sorted out and she does the accounts every morning.'

'That's no problem. If you could let me know if she is ok with that, I shall move heaven and earth to get there on time.'

The following day as Ben was leaving after his shift, he bumped into his mate Rodger who had recently been put on a different shift pattern to give him experience of work on the main section in the kitchen.

'How's your beautiful girlfriend?' Rodger was envious; she was such a good-looking girl!

'Not so bad. What about you? Are you still footloose and fancy-free?' Rodger indicated that chance would be a fine thing and that if he wasn't working, he was sleeping. They chatted about work and then Ben asked Rodger something he was not expecting. 'Rodger you're more streetwise than me. Have you ever heard of something called a speedball?

Rodger looked at Ben curiously. 'Where did you hear that? What sort of company are you keeping!'

'It's just something I heard, and you know me – I had to find out what it was.'

Rodger's face took on a more serious look. 'Ben, wherever you heard that it couldn't have been a good place. Do you know anything about recreational drugs?'

Ben wondered if it would have been better not to have mentioned it. 'Drugs are something I know next to nothing about. Aspirin and cod liver oil is about the extent of my knowledge.'

'Then why ask about something you don't understand?'

Ben was at a loss how to proceed with the conversation. 'Uh, it's just, you know, something I heard and was curious about.'

Rodger looked at his mate and frowned. 'Do you really want to know?'

Ben's response was hesitant. 'Er…yeah, just give me an idea what it is.'

Rodger took a breath. 'I don't know the full ins and outs of it, but apparently it's a mix of heroin and cocaine and it's pretty deadly if you don't know what you're doing. I had a few mates that fell into the wrong type of company and one ended up in a bad way because of that stuff. If I were you, Ben, I would stay well clear of anyone who even mentions it.'

'Could it kill you?'

'Ben, what on earth do you want to know that for?'

'Just curiosity.'

'You know what curiosity did to the cat – yes, it can kill if anyone takes enough of it. Now can we please change the subject!

Ben could see how the talk of drugs upset Rodger and he didn't want to push it, so he asked what he had been up to and who he had been working with, which Rodger gladly spoke about for the few minutes they had left before he had to start his shift.

'See you later and give Sophie a big kiss from me,' Rodger laughed as he disappeared into the hotel.

As he cycled home, things started to form in Ben's mind that gave him food for thought.

His aunt caught him as he was putting his bike away. 'Can you do me a big favour, Ben, and clear up the hedge clippings and rubbish in the garden. Maybe you could burn it, as long as it doesn't upset the neighbours.'

'No problem,' he responded, thinking it might be an opportunity to get rid of Sophie's mum's stuff.

As Ben filled the garden incinerator he kept thinking of Sophie's face when she told him about her mother. The look was one of fear, which must have been with her since she had found her mum on the floor after her overdose. He opened the biscuit tin and took out the two sachets of white powder. Those he would keep in a safe place until he decided how to either destroy them, or use them to get revenge on Jack's killer in some way.

Wrapping the remaining syringes and other paraphernalia in a cloth soaked with turpentine, he placed it in the middle of the rubbish, lit a rolled newspaper and tossed it in. There was a second or two before the whoosh of flames made Ben step further back. He watched as the flames flared and then subsided. The fire burned steadily for about thirty minutes and once he was satisfied that it had done its job he raked over the ashes. He spotted a congealed mass of melted glass containing what looked like traces of metal. Carefully removing the lump, he carried it to the farthest part of the garden where he buried it.

'Job done,' he said to himself as he tidied up and made his way back to the house to hide the tin in his bedroom for a while.

9

Sophie kept her promise and knocked on Ben's front door on the following Thursday. She was met by Ben's aunt.

'Come in, come in.' It was a warm welcome and Sophie felt at ease straightaway. 'Let me take your jacket, and then we'll go into the kitchen and I'll make us a drink.'

Sophie slid out of her jacket and then asked in a demure voice, 'What should I call you? Ben always refers to you as aunt or auntie.'

'Well, I think we are old enough to use Christian names, so you call me Sarah and I'll call you Sophie, which sounds a little like a singing or a comedy duo.' They both smiled at the thought of them being on Top of the Pops.

The time was mainly taken with talk about the garden and what Sophie was going to do with herself. They both considered they had formed a very good relationship by the time Sophie had to head home.

'Now, you must feel you can come anytime. Just let me know and I'll make sure the coffee is ready when you arrive.'

Sophie blushed a little; she had had a wonderful morning and was more determined than ever to eventually get a house and garden just like this one. 'Thank you so much,' she said, waving as she went out into the street. She felt a little light-headed, but so full of plans that she wanted to start things happening then and there, although she knew deep in her heart that it would take her a long time to achieve her dreams.

Life at the Rosegarth continued apace and both Ben and Sophie were busier than ever. Guests for both the hotel and restaurant seemed to be growing by the day. It felt like only the blink of an eye before Steyning made contact with the hotel about the provision of another meal for a private dinner party. It was planned for three weeks' time, so Burdett had to get his thinking cap on. He decided it would be good experience to let Ben come up with suggestions for the meal, which he would then finalise before proposing the menu to Steyning.

Ben was very nervous about designing a menu. It was the first time he had been put in a position where his recipes would carry the day if they were approved. He thought hard about what he would suggest as the main course, and in the end he decided on 'poussin' with garlic and rosemary, basted with white wine and garlic stock – an individual bird would be served to each person. It would be accompanied by sauté potatoes, French beans and Vichy-style carrots with a light sauce made from chicken stock.

Once he had settled on the main, he came up with trout with almonds for the fish course, and Crème Brulé for dessert. He wanted to do a professional job so he worked out the quantities of each component and priced them. Once this was put together, he nervously presented it to Burdett for comment.

'Not bad,' was his first comment. 'Do you think trout is the right thing? Not too heavy?'

'I don't think so.' Ben was sure that trout would be good.

Burdett pursed his lips and deliberated. Looking at the proposed menu again he said, 'What about some smoked trout?'

Ben didn't think it would work and explained to Burdett that if they were to use small trout and keep the butter content reasonable, it would be fairly well balanced. Burdett told Ben to leave it with him to ponder over and he would let him know his final decision the following day.

He called Ben into his small office the next morning. 'I've considered your menu and think it's worth a try. What I want you to do is cook the fish course for me tomorrow as a trial run. We have the money as Steyning is paying a little extra this time.'

The following day Ben set to work. He had purchased all the ingredients, set up his bench, took a deep breath, and began. It went well; the trout with almonds came out a treat and Burdett seemed satisfied with the way he tackled the dish. Ben's skills had certainly developed, his confidence had grown, and he was now able to feel comfortable in the kitchen no matter how hot or frantic it was. Burdett said he would draw up a full menu and then he and Ben would present it to Steyning in two days' time.

The meeting with Steyning went well. He liked the idea of trout, and the individual chickens amused him. 'There is one thing I want you to make sure of.' His voice was not critical, merely matter- of-fact. 'Don't bother too much with the wine. One bottle of red and one of white will suffice. But make sure there is plenty of water, both still and sparkling, and stick to the hors d'oeuvres that we had last time as they all liked them.'

As they left Steyning's house, Burdett patted Ben on the back. 'Well done you, we'll make a chef of you yet.' Ben's shoulders lifted, he felt good about life and couldn't wait to cook his menu, with the help of his head chef of course.

However, he soon fell into a confused state of mind. On the one hand he was excited and looking forward to using his menu for Steyning's guests, but on the other he was convinced that Steyning had been instrumental in causing his brother's death, and this gave him a conflict of interests. However, his mind and purpose were clarified by the time he went to Steyning's house for the menu to be signed off. The housekeeper, whose frosty expression thawed slightly when Ben remembered to take off his shoes, showed him in as usual. Steyning was on the phone and gestured to Ben to take a seat. Ben's eyes searched the room. It was so sumptuously furnished that he could not begin to imagine how much some of the furniture and furnishings had cost.

'How are you, young man?' Steyning said as he replaced the receiver.

'I'm very well, Mr Steyning.'

'It's Ben, isn't it?'

'Yes, sir.' Ben was at a loss as to what to call him so he stuck with 'sir' as he thought it showed respect, even though it might be misplaced.

Steyning took the menu from him. 'I hope they're not working you too hard in the kitchen, because if they are I could use a smart lad like you in my organisation.'

'That's very kind of you, Mr Steyning, but I'm happy as I am, learning my trade.'

'Mm, but you never know when things might change, so make sure you remember that I'm always on the lookout for prospective good staff.'

Ben thought for a second. 'What sort of work would it be – that's if I wanted to change? He purposely let Steyning think he was nibbling at the bait.

'Well, it would be mainly getting to know our customers, what they like and what they dislike. It would involve keeping up to date with the music of the hour and the fashions of the moment. Does that appeal to you?'

'As I've been stuck in a kitchen for the last few years my

knowledge of music is down to what I hear on the radio, and as for fashion, that's a whole world that I don't really have any idea about.'

Steyning looked thoughtfully at him. 'What I need, Ben, is someone who can get to know the kids who come to my clubs, find out what's going on in their lives – things like how and where they spend their money, what turns them on – the sort of information that could help me maximise my profits.'

Ben thought he could read between the lines of what Steyning was telling him. 'What if there is a question about the legality of their wants?'

Steyning replied with a tight smile, 'If that's what they want, we aim to please. Have a think about it and if you feel you want to earn quite a bit more than you're getting in the kitchen, come and see me.' He looked at his watch and Ben took it as a signal the meeting was over. Steyning handed over the signed menu and stood up. He walked Ben to the door, placing a hand on his shoulder. 'Don't forget to come and see me if you need a change.'

Ben said he would and made his way out of the house. He shuddered as he thought of what Steyning meant by 'giving the kids what they want'. There was no way he would ever dream of working for Steyning, but the conversation had been useful and now he was convinced that Steyning would very likely have played a part in his brother's death.

Between his meeting with Steyning and the day of the dinner party Ben went through all sorts of drama in his mind. What was he to do? He had made a promise and he intended to get revenge for his brother's death but he had no idea of just how do it.

On the designated day, Burdett and Ben took the produce for the meal to Steyning's house, and with their arms full of culinary provisions were again let in by the housekeeper who watched them remove their shoes, with some difficulty, before allowing them to step into the hall.

'You know where everything is so I'll leave you to it. Mr Steyning is out at the moment but he will be back in about an hour and a half.'

Burdett and Ben had a good four and a half hours to get the meal ready it; it might seem a long time but they had a lot to do. There wasn't just the cooking of the meal to consider, there was also the preparation, getting everything just so and keeping the customer happy. Burdett went through the courses in detail with Ben and gave him a list of things he wanted him to concentrate on. This was mainly the hard graft, leaving the more intricate touches for himself, although Ben retained responsibility for his much-practised trout dish. It was going well.

When Steyning returned, he popped his head round the kitchen door. 'Everything going to plan, gentlemen?'

Burdett looked up from his work. 'Yes, we're on time and it's looking good.'

Steyning smiled at Ben and winked, which made Ben feel conspiratorial and uncomfortable.

About an hour before the meal was due to begin, Ben said that he needed to go to the toilet, and hurriedly left the kitchen. The toilets were on the ground and first floor, and as Ben wanted to see as much of the house as he could he decided to use the one on the first-floor. He had to pass Steyning's bedroom to get there, and as he passed the open door he saw that Steyning had his clothes for the evening laid out ready for him to change into. He looked at the suit hanging on the door of the wardrobe and, remembering how Steyning had placed a sachet of white powder into the jacket pocket the last time he was there, he went up to the suit, felt in the pocket, and removed a similar white packet.

Quickly he substituted one of the sachets he had found in Sophie's mum's tin – he had brought it with him just in case the opportunity arose. Ben realised that what he was doing was desperately risky, but he could not go back as he was now more determined than ever to avenge his brother's death. But might he be committing murder? And was it murder? He cast the thought from his mind and made sure that the jacket showed no sign of being touched. How many youngsters would he be helping by taking Steyning out of the picture? More than he could imagine. He reassured himself that it didn't feel like he was doing anything wrong – it was just little packets. It wasn't as if he was going to blow Steyning's head off.

Ben returned to the kitchen just in time to see the 'bodyguard' as they now called him enter the house. His military bearing was unmistakable and his face was unsmiling. This time he wore white gloves, which amused the two chefs.

'I shall be in hall. Let me know when the food is ready to be served.' There was no please or thank you, just orders.

Burdett was now in the process of finalising the hors d'oeuvres, and once the edges of each dish had been wiped of any trace of spills, he called the bodyguard, who told him to wait until the final guest had arrived. Burdett was not pleased with the waiting as it could mean the meal would spoil. However, the guest soon arrived and the bodyguard showed them straight into the dining room.

It never struck Burdett or Ben as odd that they had never seen or even heard the guests; it was as if the bodyguard had kept them well away from them on purpose. Not that it mattered to them. As long as they approved of the food and there were no complaints, that was all that counted. The meal went well, the bodyguard moved swiftly back and forth, carrying and returning dishes, and although not a trained waiter he did an efficient job.

Around the dining table sat the same individuals – the American, Adam, at the head of the table; the Italian, Aldo; the Frenchman, Francois; the Dutchman, Christoph; and the guy from Birmingham, Joseph, together with Max Steyning. They were enjoying the meal, but more importantly they were already discussing what was to be the main topic of the evening. After the table had been cleared, each guest was given a brown leather folder containing a detailed agenda, together with a writing pad and a Parker pen. The meeting was managed by the American, and when he spoke the others gave him their full attention.

'Gentlemen, as you can see, we have a full agenda and I suggest we start without further delay.'

He was brisk and business-like in the way he conducted every agenda item. Each person would then comment or offer a report on the situation in their area of control. When it came to 'New Product Development', he took total control. He explained that there had been an innovation that could affect their business dramatically, although not for the worse, he added with a smirk. This development was about the use of synthetics, which could be highly profitable but needed careful planning. It would require a new set of people and an improved delivery system. The object of the exercise was to get the new product into the hands of as many people, particularly those between the ages of eighteen and thirty, as quickly as possible. This would create a need that they would fulfil, so, more business, more profit. Targets had been set for each area. When these were revealed, there was silence as each man tried to digest how much he was expected to achieve.

In the kitchen Burdett and Ben had just finished clearing up. The bodyguard looked in, and to Burdett's annoyance he wandered around the kitchen wearing his white gloves and inspecting various areas as if it was part of the military.

Burdett frowned and asked him, 'Are you satisfied?'

The bodyguard turned to him and smiled unpleasantly. 'It'll do.' He gave Burdett two envelopes and escorted them to the front door where they put on their shoes. The door was opened and they were quickly ushered out. As they reached the street Ben muttered that something didn't feel good in that house.

'I agree. But as long as we get paid, I'm not worried,' Burdett said as they trundled all their gear back to his car.

In the dining room the talk went on for another two hours, at which point Adam brought the proceedings to a close. He told the group that all seemed to be going in the right direction and that it would be necessary for a further meeting to ensure that the next phase of introducing the new product went without a hitch.

'The next meeting I think should not be in London but in Paris, so Francois, please make arrangements for an appropriate venue in three months' time. And that, gentlemen, I think concludes our business.' Those around the table rose and said their farewells. Adam did not go out immediately but turned to Steyning. 'Thanks for organising the meetings, Max. You have made conducting our business a lot easier than it might have been.' He opened his briefcase, and as he had done in the past, took out a small plastic bag of white powder which he passed to Steyning, who took it eagerly. Adam shook Max's hand. 'Enjoy.'

Adam left the house and got into the driving seat. Joseph, the member from Birmingham, was already in the back. Adam turned round to him and held his hand out; they shook.

'Welcome to full partnership of the European department.'

'Steyning?' Joseph asked with a raised eyebrow.

'Max is just about to retire.' With that Joseph sat back in his seat and the car pulled away.

10

Max Steyning was not as happy as he could have been. There seemed to have been an atmosphere at the meeting, something he couldn't quite put his finger on. Although the discussions had been business-like with no hint of animosity, Max felt that the others were in possession of more information than he was, particularly Joseph, the guy from Birmingham. He looked at the packet that Adam had given him and smiled to himself. *Let's go chase a dragon*, he thought, and went into his sitting room. He prepared himself for a good trip; the heroin Adam had given him in the past was always first-rate stuff.

Max did not consider himself an addict, just someone who took the white powder recreationally. He set everything up and sat in his favourite chair. The band round his arm tightened and a vein became clear, and as the needle pierced his skin he experienced what he loved – the sudden surge of success and happiness and euphoria that flooded him – he had reached for the stars and they were in his hands. Unexpectedly a pall of confusion and uncertainty drifted over his senses and he found it difficult to breath. He looked down at his arm and tried to rip off the band of rubber. His breaths became rasping and laboured and he felt an overwhelming loss of contact with reality. It was then that his world came crashing down as his breathing failed. His chest gave one last heave and Max Steyning lay dead in his chair.

The following morning, a Sunday, an unmarked small van pulled up outside Steyning's house. The bodyguard climbed out and from the rear of the van removed a large box which he carried to the door. He was wearing gloves, which this time were not his fancy white ones but heavy-duty rubber gloves, which made his handling of the key a little awkward. Once inside, he opened the box. It was full of cleaning materials. He walked down the hall and into the kitchen and began his task. Although Burdett and Ben had cleaned everywhere thoroughly before they left, he went over every surface making sure everything that had been touched was wiped clean. From there he went into the dining room and cleaned every surface with a bleach solution.

Opposite the dining room was Steyning's study containing a desk with a comfortable chair, visitors' chairs, two four-drawer filing cabinets and a two-drawer one. He tried to open the filing cabinets, but they were locked. From a side pocket he took out a small leather case and unzipped it. It contained a selection of lock picks. He studied the cabinet locks, selected a pick and within forty seconds the filing cabinet was unlocked, the drawers gliding open on their runners. He looked quickly at a series of file holders, each labelled, then started to remove each one. He placed the files into strong plastic bags. It needed six to hold all the files and they were quite a weight. The bodyguard picked up two of the bags and carried them out to his van. The road was clear; Sunday mornings were not busy, especially in this area where most people were taking a leisurely approach to possibly their only day off.

Although it took him three trips to load the bags into the van, he was sure he had attracted very little attention, if any. He proceeded to check the desk, removing anything that might indicate the business that Max Steyning had been involved in.

After one further trip to the van, he was satisfied. He then backed into the hall cleaning any traces of his footsteps, and glanced into the sitting room where he could see Steyning slumped in his chair. He closed the door, taking care to wipe everything he touched.

In the hall and toilet every surface got the same treatment. After two hours he was happy with his work and confident he had cleaned everywhere that could have been touched by the guests the previous evening. Finally wiping the front door inside and out, he closed it, clicked the lock shut and made his way back to the van.

Max Steyning's house keeper opened the front door on the Monday morning as usual and went in. She was surprised to smell a faint tang of bleach in the air, but surmised it may have been the chefs cleaning up after a spillage. She looked into the dining room and again noticed the faint smell, although all seemed in very good shape after the dinner party – she had half expected some mess. She went from the dining room into the sitting room and saw Max Steyning's body contorted in his chair, a terrible look on his face, his lips blue and his eyes – she had to look away. She didn't scream, she just shook with fear. She could see Steyning's arm and the needle on the floor and thought he must surely be dead, but she didn't know for sure so she picked up the phone and dialled 999.

She met the two ambulance men at the door and took them into the sitting room.

'I don't know if he's dead or alive,' she told them. They checked for signs of life but could find none. 'Have you called the police?'

The housekeeper shook her head. 'Why would I?'

The ambulance driver said it looked to him like a drug

overdose and that anything connected with drugs was automatically passed to the police. 'This is something we come across occasionally and the police have to be informed.'

'Do what you must,' she said, still shaking.

He looked at his partner. 'Go with her into the other room and I'll radio for the police.'

It didn't take long for the police to arrive. Two constables in uniform and a plain clothes detective appeared at the door where they were met by the ambulance driver. A good look at the dead man and the state the body was in, together with the syringe, the packet of white powder and the length of elastic, plus Steyning's distorted face, led him to the very rapid conclusion that the man had taken an overdose: of what, he didn't know, but his guess would be heroin.

Within twenty minutes the house was swarming with police in various guises. Two further plain clothes detectives arrived and after consulting their colleagues, went into the sitting room to talk to the housekeeper.

'How are you feeling?' the most senior of them asked her.

'I'm not sure, I can't stop shaking.'

'Do you feel up to answering a few questions?'

She squeezed her hands together to stop them from trembling. 'Yes, but I don't know if I can help you. I've only just got here – I'm the housekeeper.'

'The inspector will be with you shortly,' he told her.

Peter Russell of the Drug Squad looked around the room and satisfied himself that this was no regular overdose situation. He called one of the uniformed officers to the doorway and gave instructions not to let anyone in unless he authorised it.

'Chris, get onto the station, we need forensics out here pdq.' Chris Stamford nodded and went to his car to radio in for the

SOCO to attend. Peter Russell then went back to the housekeeper to ask her for her version of events. He pulled up a chair to where she was sitting and sat in front of her.

'First things – I'm Detective Inspector Peter Russell, and the gentleman you saw in the other room is my sergeant, Chris Stamford. Let's start with your name and where you live.'

She looked up at the inspector. 'I'm Jenny Prentice and I live at Flat 1A, 114 Coningham Road, W12.' He knew the area. It was a reasonable place to live and not too far away from where she worked.

'Do you live alone?'

'Yes, my husband left some time ago.'

'Has he passed on?'

'No, he just upped and left about ten years back,' she snapped. 'What happened to him I don't know and quite honestly I don't want to know.' Her manner was one of loathing when she spoke of her husband. She looked back at the inspector. 'Do you know what's happened here?'

'That's just what I'm trying to find out.'

He then asked what her role was in the house and she explained to him that she was sort of chief cook and bottle washer. 'I come in six days a week and clean, but I do only a half day on a Saturday as Mr Steyning has …had… visitors Saturday afternoons.'

'What sort of visitors?' Peter Russell was interested in anyone who might have been in contact with the dead man.

'All sorts. They ranged from youngsters to middle-aged men. I never saw any women visitors. If there were any they must have arrived after I left.'

'Did he have any last weekend that you know of?'

'Yes, he had some sort of business meeting. He had them

every so often. Apparently he entertained some important business people, but I never knew their names or got to see any of them.'

'How did he entertain them, and do you know how many there were?'

She held her head back slightly as if she was trying to remember all that had happened the previous week. 'I think he had about six or seven guests. That was how the table was arranged in here and he brought in outside caterers to prepare the meal.'

'Do you know who these caterers were?'

'Oh yes.' She was pleased she knew exactly who they were. 'They came from a hotel near here. I think it's called the Rosegarth. It's very posh and very expensive. He had two chefs come and cook the meal here. I saw them several times. Had to keep reminding them to take off their shoes. They also came previously to discuss the menu before the meal. I overheard them talking about the courses and how the menu would be made up.'

'Can you remember the names of the chefs?'

'I think the main man was called Burdett. I can't recall the other chef's name. He was young. It could have been Bert or something like that.'

Chris Stamford appeared in the doorway. 'SOCO has arrived.'

'Thanks, Chris.' He turned back to the housekeeper. 'Thanks for that, Mrs Prentice, you have been very helpful.' He looked at her hands. They had stopped shaking and she looked more in control of her emotions. 'I may need to speak to you again. Would that be alright?'

'That's fine. If I can be of help finding out what happened to Mr Steyning please get in touch.'

'Do you feel well enough to get home by yourself, or would you like me to organise a car to take you?'

'A lift home would be very welcome. I do feel rather unsteady still.' Her surly gaze softened a little.

'That's no problem. I will get one of the constables to drive you.' He looked round the door asked the constable to give Mrs Prentice a lift home.

As the housekeeper left, Peter Russell stopped one on the SOCO team. 'Any joy on how this happened?'

The white-clad individual looked at Russell and shrugged. 'It's definitely an overdose, but of what we can't say until we get him back to the lab.'

'Will you take care of the removal of the body?'

'Leave it to us and I'll be in contact with you about the post-mortem. There is something strange about this one.'

'Such as?' Peter queried with a lift of his eyebrows.

'It seems that he died just after injecting himself, which is not usually the way these things go. It may be that he used a very powerful amount of heroin, but we can find no significant signs of that. Let's hope the p m will give us more information. I'll also take the syringe back for analysis and see what he used.'

Chris Stamford came from the kitchen. 'Nothing in there, it's spotless. I can't even find any trace of the meal they had.'

'Better get it written up, and if SOCO have finished, get the body released. Do we have a next of kin?'

'That's the other interesting thing. There seems to be absolutely nothing referring to family or friends.'

Russell shook his head; this was not proving to be a simple case. 'See if you can find any bank details or name of a solicitor, then after SOCO have finished we'll go over the place again, inch by inch. There must be something.'

'Will do.' Chris Stamford went to join the SOCO team who were discussing the material found. He could understand most of what was being said but was lost when it came to chemical analysis. The pathologist was unsure what drug Steyning had used and said it was something he had not come up against before and he was keen to get samples back to the lab.

Things went smoothly and the body was removed, leaving Peter Russell to make his own search. He started at the front door and went through every cupboard and drawer he could find. Everything was clean and neatly stored and, most annoyingly for Peter, there was no correspondence other than the plans and bills relating to the meal. There were no cheque stubs, and no letters from the council or service suppliers. So where were all the bills? He couldn't find anything to do with the telephone or any vehicle, just nothing, and Peter knew that nobody lived like that.

As the SOCO team were about to leave, one of the team approached Peter. 'There was another odd thing. He had a sachet of what look to be drugs in his jacket pocket. It was unopened, so we will be having a close look at that as well.'

'Let me know what you find as soon as you can.'

The white-suited figure nodded and left with his team mates.

'Chris!' Peter called out.

Chris appeared. 'What's next on the agenda?'

'Get the boys from the office to go over the scene with a fine-tooth comb, and then I think we'll take a trip to a very fine hotel, don't you?'

Peter had got directions from the constable on the door, who knew the area well. He had also told Peter that it was a very high-class hotel used by a lot of the embassies that were scattered around the area. 'It's not far, about ten minutes on foot, so I think a breath of fresh air will do us good. Come on, let's walk.'

The pair were of similar height, around six foot, but of the two Peter had the slighter build. He had the appearance of someone who kept himself in good physical shape. He had a confident manner and was smartly dressed with mid-brown hair neat and well cut. A straight nose sat in the centre of a face that wasn't use to that much laughter, especially where work was concerned. Overall, his features were clean and well defined, with a somewhat pale complexion and blue eyes which took in more than most.

Chris Stamford on the other hand had a broad figure, a rolling gait, and a mop of tousled hair framing a rugby-battered face that carried the scars of many matches lost and won against heavy odds. His tan was a result of time spent on the training field and lengthy runs trying to build up his stamina – and get rid of hangovers.

'How did the match go?' Peter asked with mild curiosity.

'It was pretty tough.'

'Did you win?' Peter asked, dreading the answer.

'No, we lost on the field – but we gave them a good thrashing in the bar!'

Peter had from time to time been in the Metropolitan Police Rugby Club bar; it was not a place for the faint-hearted.

'Did you score?'

Chris gave a grunt. 'You must be joking. The nearest I ever get to the try line is when we're picking up the ball after our opposition have scored.'

They turned left and could see their destination.

The hotel entrance had double glass doors. Peter expected to see a doorman but none was in evidence. They walked into the foyer and could see why people had said it was high-class. The furnishings and décor were of a standard very rarely seen on a policeman's salary. Peter thought he might have to close Chris's mouth as they approached the reception desk. They were greeted by a very attractive young lady. Chris turned to Peter and made a gesture of approval that was all too familiar.

'Can I help you, gentlemen?' The young woman, smartly dressed in the hotel livery, wore a gold badge clearly showing her name, 'Sophie'.

Peter stepped forward. 'We're from the Metropolitan Police. I'm Detective Inspector Russell and this is Detective Sergeant Stamford. We would like to speak to someone about a catering commission that your hotel undertook for a gentleman by the name of Steyning. Can you help us?'

'I'll fetch the manageress for you.'

She left reception, disappearing through a door to the rear and returning within a minute followed by an attractive woman of about thirty-five, extremely well dressed, with eyes that would make most men swoon. They certainly had that effect on Chris Stamford.

'How can I help you, gentlemen?' Her voice matched the rest of her. It had a slight huskiness that was very appealing.

'I'm Inspector Peter Russell and this is Sergeant Chris Stamford. We understand you carried out some catering for a Mr Steyning last Saturday and we would like to speak to all those who may have been involved.'

The manageress was efficient in both movement and speech. 'I'll check the bookings. I won't be long. If you would like to take a seat and if you would like tea or coffee, let Sophie know and she will arrange it.' She disappeared back into her office.

'Tea or coffee, gentlemen?' Sophie's voice had softness about it, and *very nice it is too*, thought Chris Stamford.

Peter Russell answered for both of them 'Nothing at the

moment, Miss, thank you.' Chris looked disappointed. He fancied a nice cup of hotel coffee. It wasn't often he got the chance. Perhaps later.

The manageress returned. She smiled at them. 'I have checked and we did carry out some off-site catering last Saturday for a Mr Steyning. The best person to speak to regarding this particular job would be our head chef, David Burdett.' She looked up at Peter who noticed that her eyes were an unusual mix of green and hazel. 'Give me a moment and I'll see if he's available.' She picked up the phone and tapped in a number. 'Is Mr Burdett there?' she asked. There was a slight pause, then, 'Ah, David, I have two police officers who would like to have a word with you. Can I send them through?' She listened, then added, 'Ok, two minutes and I'll get Sophie to bring them to your office.'

11

David Burdett was curious as to why the police would want to speak to him. He finished what he was doing and straightened the papers on his desk.

Sophie appeared in the doorway. 'Mr Burdett, these are the two policemen Annabel spoke to you about.'

Both Peter and Chris made a mental note of the manager's name, thinking it might come in useful later – for other interests than just their enquiries.

Burdett stood to greet the two detectives. 'How do you do, I'm David Burdett, head chef.'

Peter Russell reached out and shook Burdett's hand. 'I'm Peter Russell and this is Chris Stamford.'

Burdett gestured to the two men to take a seat. 'What can I do for you gentlemen?'

Peter began, 'We would like to ask you about the outside catering you did for a Mr Steyning last Saturday.'

Burdett looked worried. 'Is there a problem?

'I'm afraid it looks as if Mr Steyning took an overdose on Saturday night and died shortly after.' Peter looked at Burdett for a reaction. There was a look of utter astonishment on his face.

'We were there on Saturday from about 3 pm until we finished, which must have been around eleven or half past. We aimed as always to get the meal ready on time, and once it was finished Mr Steyning made payment and then we left.'

'You say 'we'– not just you, then?'

'No, I had one of my commis chefs with me.'

'Is he at work now? If he is, we will want to speak to him.'

'Yes, Ben's in the kitchen now. Shall I fetch him?'

Peter thought that one story at a time would be enough. 'Not at the moment. I'd like to hear your account of the night first.'

David Burdett took a deep breath and related how they had compiled a menu for Steyning, and once he approved it, they bought the necessary items, went to his house and prepared the dinner for him and his guests. He explained how he and Ben were told to keep in the kitchen and not to enter the dining room at any time.

'How did you get the food to the table?' Peter asked.

'That was the odd part. The guests brought their own sort of waiter though he seemed more like a bodyguard, which is what Ben and I called him.'

Peter asked for a more detailed description of the so-called 'bodyguard'.

Burdett leaned back in his chair with his hand to his forehead. 'It was a funny set up. This chap who turned up to act as waiter – in no way was he trained for the job – reminded both Ben and me of an American soldier – you know, the ones you see on the news about Vietnam.' He went on to explain to the two detectives how the bodyguard said very little, just made sure they kept to the kitchen.

'Did you get his name or hear him discuss anything with the guests?'

'Sorry, no, he just took the plates of food into the dining room then stood in the hallway with the door to the kitchen open so that he could see when the dishes were ready. And he checked on how we cleaned the kitchen before we left.'

Chris Stamford jumped in. 'Did you happen to see how the guests arrived and departed?'

'Afraid not. We were in the kitchen when they arrived and we left before them.'

Peter asked, a little exasperated, 'So you didn't see a single one of the guests except for Steyning and the person you call the bodyguard. Is that right?'

'Yes, that's all we saw.'

'Can you let me have all the paperwork relating to the meal – that's bills, receipts, and menus, anything that was used that day or that night, please.' Peter leaned forward. 'I'd like to see the young chef who was with you now.'

Burdett went to the office door and called out for Ben. 'He'll be with us in a sec.' He sat back down and asked Peter Russell exactly what had happened. Peter shook his head and said that they didn't know much but they were trying to build a picture from all the information they were getting.

There was a knock and Ben came in.

'This is Ben. He's the commis chef who was with me on Saturday.'

It was a nervous Ben who entered Burdett's office. He had had very little to do with the police since the death of his brother and looked anxious and embarrassed.

'Take a seat, Ben. I'm Detective Inspector Peter Russell and this,' he pointed towards his colleague, 'is Detective Sergeant Chris Stamford.'

Ben sat down looking at Burdett and wondering what was coming next. He felt fear starting to well up inside him. Had he killed a man? He was about to find out.

'Ben, we have just informed Mr Burdett of the death of Mr

Steyning, the gentleman you catered for last Saturday,' began Peter Russell. 'I want you to think carefully and tell me exactly what part you played and everything you saw during your time in the house. Is that ok?'

Ben glanced at Burdett, who nodded. 'I arrived at the house at around 3 o'clock and started as soon as we got into the kitchen. I started the prep for the meal beginning with the items for the hors d'oeuvres and then went on to start preparing the fish. I just carried out the jobs that needed to be done the way Mr Burdett had instructed me when we had discussed the menu.' Ben found it difficult to hold his nerve and tried hard to keep a picture of his brother in his mind.

Peter Russell didn't want to stop Ben's flow but neither did he want him to miss out anything, so he stopped Ben and asked him to describe what he had seen when he entered Steyning's house. Ben was a little flustered, but went through his arrival before he started in the kitchen. His account was similar to Burdett's. Russell was satisfied and asked Ben to carry on.

'We cooked or prepared the dishes and the tall guy we called the bodyguard took them through to the dining room. We never left the kitchen except when we went to the toilet.'

'When you went to the toilet did you see or hear anything, anything at all?'

'The toilet is only two doors from the kitchen and it's in the opposite direction to the dining room.' Ben didn't want to go into the reasons he had for using the first-floor toilet, so left that out of his story.

'Ok.' It was clear to Russell that the two chefs had been carefully kept away from anything that had taken place in the dining room.

'Ben, I understand that you met with Steyning when you

took the menu for his approval, is that right?'

Ben began to feel desperately uncomfortable. What was he going to say? He could feel the palms of his hands becoming damp with sweat. 'Yes, I took the menu to Mr Steyning for his final approval and sign off.'

Russell thought that this might lead somewhere but he could also see Ben's reaction to questioning was not good. 'Tell me, Ben, what did Steyning talk about when you came to see him?'

Ben squirmed a little in his chair. 'He mainly talked about himself and how he had started from being a nobody to becoming quite a wealthy man.'

This was getting interesting. 'What did he tell you?'

Ben tried to get his words right. He didn't want to end up being involved in Steyning's death if he could help it. 'He told me how he had started as a sort of floor man and would spend most of his time talking to the customers, especially those who came to the clubs to dance and listen to music.'

'What sort of things did he talk to them about?'

'He said it was just making sure they were alright and if there was anything he could get them.'

'What sort of things did he get for them, Ben?'

'Well, he said drinks and stuff, but that's about all he said.'

'What do you think he meant by 'stuff'?'

'I have no idea. I didn't ask many questions. Mr Burdett had warned me that he could talk a lot, so I kept quiet most of the time and just listened.'

'Ben, I want you to have a really good think about what Steyning told you and come down to the station and have another talk with Sergeant Stamford. Can you do that?'

'When would you like see me?'

Chris Stamford looked at his boss. 'How about the day after

tomorrow? I'm sure Mr Burdett would let you take a couple of hours off to help us.' He looked at Burdett, who nodded.

'No problem,' he said.

Peter Russell stood up and held out his hand towards the head chef.

'Thanks for your time and for letting Ben come down to the station. We may need to discuss this further, so is it ok to come here or would you prefer the station?'

Burdett shook Russell's hand and said that at the hotel would be fine and at least they would know where to find him as he would be in the kitchen most of the time.

'Ben will show you back to reception.'

Ben led the two detectives through the kitchen and into the foyer, where he could see Sophie behind the desk. She spotted him and gave a little wave. He smiled and turned to head back to the kitchen.

'I'll see you the day after tomorrow, Ben, at the station,' said Chris Stamford. 'If you have any difficulties give me a ring.' Ben nodded and made his way back to his work station.

For the next two days Ben could not settle. Nights were the worst and sleep eluded him. Should he tell the police what he had done? If he did, would he be held responsible for Steyning's death? It would ruin his life in so many ways – his job, his relationship with Sophie, and what would it do to his aunt and uncle's reputation? No, he would keep his mouth shut and only admit to placing the packet of drugs in Steyning's pocket if there was no alternative.

His aunt became concerned. He was off his food and she could see he was troubled. She asked him if anything was wrong but received only a grunt in response. She thought it must be to do with his relationship with Sophie, but hoped it wasn't. Two days later Ben left home to go to the police station in a state of barely-controlled panic. He kept telling himself to keep his head and not make a complete idiot of himself.

On his arrival he asked for Sergeant Stamford. Chris Stamford didn't really know what he was supposed to get from Ben, but he would have a go at getting more details of Ben's conversation during the time they had spent together talking over the menu for the dinner parties. He met Ben at the front desk and took him into the back office and then into an interview room.

'Ben, let's not hang around, we're both busy men. Can you tell me anything that you may have remembered about your discussions with Mr Steyning?'

Ben could see that the man sitting opposite him was not in a mood for prevaricating, so he went over his movements and the conversations he had had with Steyning. Stamford was very interested in what had been said about Steyning's role in the running of clubs, especially any recent details, but Ben told him that Steyning had only talked about what he had done at the beginning of his career in the clubs. He did reveal that Steyning had offered him a job in one of his clubs. This focused Stamford's attention, which was beginning to drift.

'Tell me about the offer. Was it just talk or was he serious?'

'I think he was serious, but I told him that although it sounded good, I was happy in the kitchen.'

'What did he say would be involved in working for him?'

'He wasn't too specific. He said it would be similar to his job when he first started. He would expect me to mix with the dancers and drinkers in the clubs and get information about their likes and dislikes so that he could capitalise on them.'

'Did he say what these likes and dislikes might involve?'

'No, he was pretty vague on that. I thought it was just to do with drinks and the type of music played and possibly any bands that the clubs put on.'

'Think carefully, Ben, did he ever mention pills or drugs of any description?'

'He may have said a little about his early days when pills were easily obtainable in some clubs, but that's all.'

Ben thought he may have said too much so he tried to get away from that subject and asked if Stamford knew how Steyning had died. Stamford rubbed his chin and felt the stubble from his bad shave that morning. His mind seemed to be elsewhere.

'We know he was killed with drugs but are not quite sure what sort, and our search team could only find one simple small sachet, unopened, of some sort of heroin and cocaine mix in his house, and that was in his jacket pocket.

'Could that have killed him – if he'd opened it?'

'Our lab boys think it could have if he had taken it with something else, like a fair quantity of alcohol, but considering there wasn't much alcohol in his system, that is highly unlikely. Anyway, it was not the same as the stuff that killed him so rapidly.'

Ben's body physically slumped in his chair.

'Are you ok? You look a bit rough.'

'Oh, I've just had a few bad nights. I may have been overdoing it at work. We put in very long hours, you know.'

Stamford was a little surprised that Ben had asked questions about Steyning's death, but put it down to the curiosity of youth. 'Thanks for coming in, Ben. I'll see you out.'

As they walked towards the front desk, Stamford again asked Ben to think carefully about all that was said between him and Steyning and that if the slightest thing came to mind to contact him straightaway. Ben was feeling so relieved he almost skipped out of the police station. He told himself that he was in the clear. The sachet of drugs he had placed in Steyning's pocket had not been used, and he breathed a sigh of relief.

At their regular morning briefing Peter Russell went over the case with his team. 'In my mind this incident with Steyning is a lot more complex than meets the eye. We have interviewed those that were in the house during and before the incident but cannot seem to get any concrete information on just who Steyning was or who he was involved with. Chris, did you find out any more from the young lad?'

Chris got up. 'Not really. I went through the time he had spent with Steyning but not much came of it, although it appears that Steyning had been involved in the club scene for some considerable time. He also offered the lad a job, being a sort of researcher into what the customers wanted. Now that could have been anything from lemonade to heroin or pills or whatever else might be coming on the market. It gives me an uneasy feeling about this character.'

One of the DCs said that the SOCO team had brought in something that they had initially missed and thought it might be of interest. He held up a clear plastic bag containing three name tags of the sort meant for files. They had been originally attached to files and had got stuck in the joins of the filing cabinet drawers. He laid them out on the desk: Inferno; Flames; Smokies.

Russell asked if anyone knew of clubs with those names. From the general chorus, it appeared they were well known about five years ago but seemed to have fallen out of fashion.

'Anything else?' Russell asked. Another DC told the group that they were still following up on any possible links to the continent or the USA, but it was slow going.

'Chris, can you try to find out as much as you can about these so-called clubs and take Eddy with you. Phil and Ray, just keep on digging. There must be something we can start to build a picture on. Ok, let's get on with it.'

He turned to Stamford. 'If you get anything, let me know. I'm going to have another talk with the chef and the manageress at the Rosegarth. I want to see how long Steyning has been a customer of the hotel and if he has used it to accommodate any guests or friends.'

Chris Stamford made a note of the three names and went with Eddy to the Records section. A giant of a man greeted them. God only knew how he got a job in Records as he could barely fit through the door.

'What can we do for you?'

'We want to go clubbing and thought you might be able to give us some info on these three names.'

The big man smiled and quipped, 'Aren't you a bit long in the tooth to go tripping the light fantastic?'

'Me? Too old? I'm still a spring chicken compared to most of you in here.'

It was good friendly banter and Chris wanted to keep it that way. He did not want to get on the wrong side of the man mountain. The big constable turned to a bank of drawers and started to look through them.

'I thought you were getting some new-fangled computers to do all this searching for you, Harry?'

Harry grinned good-naturedly. 'Not yet,' he said, 'it's still good old finger power.' He took out some cards, adding 'Is this what you're after?' He brought over three index cards. The first was headed up 'Inferno' and had red lines across it.

'What does that mean?' Chris pointed at the lines.

'It means, dear friend, that it no longer exists. You won't believe this but it seems to have burnt down. Now *there's* irony for you.'

Chris turned to Eddy. 'Cross that one off the list.'

The big constable held out two more cards each of which contained a few details. Eddy took down the clubs' addresses.

'Thanks, Harry, you've saved us quite a lot of time and shoe leather.'

'Any time, mate. We're always open to good customers. Have fun and don't get carried away.'

12

As Chris left the records office, Peter Russell was approaching the Rosegarth. He wanted to find out if there were any further links between Steyning and the hotel. He was intrigued too by the manageress and the way she had looked at him. As he walked towards the reception desk he could see the young girl, Sophie, behind the desk, and just as he was about to ask if he could see the manageress, she opened the door to her office and spotted him.

'Hello, Inspector, what brings you back? More questions, I suppose?' He couldn't get over the way she looked at him, with a slight pout; her lips were full, and a line of white teeth could be seen just behind them. He had to mentally shake himself back into reality.

'A few more questions, it shouldn't take long.'

Annabel Stewart could tease most men and she didn't hold back – in fact she enjoyed it, but somehow this man held more of her interest. 'I'm just about to have my break. Would you like to join me?'

Peter wondered if she was flirting with him, but dismissed it as unlikely. 'Erm, yes, that would be good.'

'This way.' She led him into the restaurant. Peter looked around. It felt very classy. The circular tables were covered with silk-figured damask tablecloths and there was a glass vase of fresh flowers in the centre of each one – not the tatty plastic ones they had in the police canteen. She pulled out a chair and sat down, smoothing her skirt elegantly. 'Have you ever visited our restaurant, Peter?'

That she had remembered his name, for some reason made him feel uneasy. 'I think it's rather out of my price range.'

'Surely not for a special occasion – a birthday or perhaps an anniversary? You could treat your wife to a wonderful night out by bringing her here.'

'That would be difficult as I don't have a wife.' He felt he was playing into her hands.

'In that case we would have to see if we couldn't find you a suitable partner for the evening.'

Peter thought, *God, she's doing it again* as he noticed a wicked smile cross her face. He was not that comfortable in female company because he found that his mind simply could not cope with small talk. He was pragmatic in his thinking and his job filled most of his waking hours. There had been several encounters with the opposite sex, but nothing ever came of them. He just could not seem to converse in a way that interested women. He had to admit to himself as well that he had never encountered a woman like this before, and to be truthful, he was a little afraid. She brought him back to ground level.

'I've asked Sophie to invite David Burdett to join us. Is there anyone else you would like to speak to?'

'Actually, *you* might to be able to help me. I need to know if this Mr Steyning had any previous dealings with the hotel. Did he, for instance, have any friends or colleagues stay as guests, and if he did when and for how long?'

'I'll have a look through our records and let you know ... or would you like to call again?'

She's doing it again! he thought. Aloud he said, 'If you can't get hold of me in the office, leave a message. I can always call and collect any information you may have found.' He was rambling and he didn't know why.

'Anything else?'

'Um, yes, it might be helpful if I could have another word with – Ben, I think his name is – the young lad from the kitchen.'

'That's no problem.'

David Burdett appeared from the kitchen and took a seat at the table.

'David will arrange for Ben to see you.'

'What can I do for you, Inspector?'

Peter tried to focus on what he wanted from Burdett but his thoughts and eyes kept going back to the woman sitting opposite him. Luckily the young girl from reception appeared. 'Annabel, there are some customers who wish to discuss various arrangements with you.'

'I'm so sorry, gentlemen, I shall have to leave you. I am sure you will be able to get all the information you want from David and Ben. And don't forget, Detective Inspector, you are always welcome here at the Rosegarth.' She gave him a teasing look, rose to her feet, adjusted her collar, and headed back to the reception area, followed by Sophie.

Peter let out a sigh of relief. 'That's some manager you've got there,' he said to Burdett.

'You're not kidding, she's one of a kind.'

Peter rubbed his eyes. 'I need to know any background you can give me because we seem to be coming up with nothing more than fragments of Mr Steyning's life. For instance, did you ever meet anyone else when you discussed meals with him, or did he ever come here for meals with anyone?'

Burdett could only reiterate what he had told Russell before, that they had previously carried out some catering for Steyning but had never really seen his guests. One thing he was sure about was that his guests very likely came from far and wide.

'What makes you so sure of that?'

Burdett explained how some of the items on the various menus had included elements from Europe, some from Asia, and one or two that could only be to satisfy the American palate.

'But you never saw or heard Steyning discussing anything with them?'

'No, sorry, I can't even remember seeing them – I guess they were a very secretive bunch. But he paid handsomely so I didn't really care about who he entertained.'

Peter paused. 'Could you ask Ben to come and have a chat?'

'Sure, I'll get him for you.'

'Just before you go, I have to ask if you have seen any signs of drug use in the hotel, either among staff or guests?'

Burdett stopped for a second. 'I haven't seen or heard of drugs in the hotel, but that's not to say it doesn't go on. We have many rooms and sometimes guests have peculiar habits. Not just drugs-related either. Perhaps the door staff can help.'

'That was my next stop after a quick chat with Ben.'

'You don't need me to stay. I must get back to the kitchen.'

'No, you go, and thanks for your time.'

Peter saw Ben approaching. 'Grab a seat, Ben, just a couple of quick questions.'

Ben felt a lot more self-confident since speaking to Sergeant Stamford and knowing that he could not have been responsible for Steyning's death. Russell could see that Ben was more relaxed than the last time they spoke. 'Ben, I know you've had a session with Sergeant Stamford, but I want to ask two questions

One, have you ever heard or seen any sign of drugs in the hotel, either by the staff or guests? And two, have you ever been approached by anyone from outside the hotel regarding drugs?'

Ben shook his head. 'No, I've never seen anything like that in the hotel. Drugs scare the life out of me and I think I would run a mile if anyone suggested anything like that to me.'

'What about your fellow chefs – do you think they might perhaps take something to help them through the long hours you guys work?'

'If they do, I don't know about it. I try to keep myself to myself and get on with my job.'

'I understand you go to college on a regular basis,' Russell continued. 'What about there, have you ever come across drugs at college?' Ben replied he had heard talk of uppers and downers, but he really didn't want to know. He had seen some of the students get kicked off their course for alcohol and possible drug abuse, but he just didn't want anything to jeopardise his future.

'Ok, Ben, thanks for your time.'

Ben headed back to work feeling good, that life was getting better again.

Peter Russell went back to reception and asked Sophie how many doormen they had and was surprised when she said they didn't have any. The hotel employed bell boys, but no out-front door staff. There were two smartly attired bell boys in the foyer who stood waiting for any instructions from the reception desk. Peter asked Sophie what hours they worked. She told him there were six shifts altogether; two earlies, two lates and two off, and offered to ask Annabel to give him their shift pattern.'

Peter thought quickly. 'No, I think that will do for the moment. I'll ask Chris Stamford to have a word with them later.'

He left the hotel and was not a happy man. He had gained

very little useful information and had few avenues to follow up. He hoped that his sergeant had had more luck.

Chris Stamford had been given the job of investigating the clubs whose names they found in Steyning's filing cabinet. He climbed into the driver's seat of his car and Eddy Pullen stretched his legs before getting into the passenger's seat.

'Ok, Eddy you're the navigator today. Which way do we go?' Eddy had some idea of the addresses but needed some back-up, so he carefully checked with his A to Z and managed to give clear directions to his sergeant without getting lost. They arrived at their first port of call, 'Flames'. It was not a regular haunt of either man and definitely not the sort of place where Chris Stamford would want be seen, although better than he had expected. They went to the main entrance, which was locked and probably didn't open until around 9 pm. There were two bells, clearly marked 'Office' and 'Deliveries'. Eddy pushed the Office bell and waited. It took two or three minutes for the door to open and a figure to appear.

'Yes, can I help you?' The voice came from a man in his late thirties. His appearance was not what Chris had expected. He had a round, rather plump, clean-shaven face, and was casually dressed in a pair of blue trousers and a white shirt, open at the neck.

Chris held out his warrant card. 'Police. Can we have a word?'

'Of course. Members of the Metropolitan Police are always welcome in my establishment. Come in. What can I do for you? I'm Geoffrey Bicker. I run this place, or should I say try to run it.' He led them into the main dance area of the club, then up two flights of stairs to an office. It was comfortable, relatively neat, and smacked of an efficiently run operation. 'Take a seat, please.'

Chris studied the man. His gestures were relaxed, yet there seemed to be some hesitancy in his manner. 'We are looking into the running of various entertainment clubs in the Met area and would like to get some background information on their management. I'd like you to tell me how this club is run – things like who owns it, is it a part of a larger group of clubs, what sort of clientele you have, their age group and so on.'

Once Geoffrey Bicker got started there was no stopping him. He explained how he had been enticed into the club world by some very good advertising for a start-up small business scheme, had seen an opportunity which he could not resist, had been in possession of some savings and thought it a very good investment. It had been sold to him as a 'franchise', which in essence meant he would run the club and be responsible for its profits for an annual franchise fee payable to his sponsors. He had no problem it getting in on the action, he said.

'I attended a meeting with around ten others. We were told exactly what our investment would be and that the returns would be down to how we each managed our own business. It was just what I was looking for so I signed up without a second thought.

Chris looked around at the posters of groups on the wall.

'Do *you* book the acts that appear here?'

'Yes. Well, I say I do, but I have made contact with agents and do it through them.' He carried on without any prompting and the detail that he came out with was very interesting. He told them he had virtually a free hand; he hired and fired staff, fixed the entrance fee, chose what went behind the bar, and the price that drinks were sold for.

'How many staff do you have?'

'Oh, I have regular core staff, but I also have a number of part-time staff who lend a hand when we have a big night planned. I suppose all told there must be a dozen or so if you include the part-timers. Plus two doormen.'

Eddy chipped in, 'Doormen, what do they do?'

'They keep the entrance clear of undesirables, and make sure we get a good mix of male and female.'

'Do you get much trouble?'

Geoffrey hesitated. 'Not much really, mostly just the occasional fight, which is mainly due to drink, but nothing that the doormen can't handle.'

Chris took over the conversation. 'Can you tell me who actually owns the club?'

'I only know that the profits are paid into an account with the Westminster Bank. I did get a visit very early on from a gentleman whose name sounded German or something.'

'Was it Steyning?'

'I think that was it, or something very like it.'

'Did you have much to do with that individual?'

'Not much, but there was one strange thing. I didn't tell you about all the staff I had working in the club because two of them were foisted upon me by Steyning. He said they were marketing agents placed in all his clubs to assess a club's future needs.'

'Their names, or any other details?' Chris wanted to get on and was becoming a little irritated.

'I only knew them as Charlie and Henry. I didn't speak to them much – they were a couple of loners, mostly ignoring the rest of the staff and concentrating on the customers.'

Eddy let out a small snort. 'Charlie and Henry. I wonder if their names related to anything else.'

'Mr Bicker, tell me all that you know about these two characters, and in particular where I can get hold of them.'

Geoffrey Bicker was getting very nervous and beginning to

wonder what he had got himself into; after all, he was only trying to run a business. Stamford could see the anxiety in his eyes and wondered what it was that was upsetting him.

'I don't have their addresses. As I said before, they kept themselves apart from the staff and me. I tried to get to know them but they shunned any move I made in that direction.'

'Nevertheless,' Stamford was insistent, 'I want you to give my colleague a very full description of these two and every bit of information you have – how they dressed, who they spoke to, what time they arrived and left, and most importantly whether you saw them make any deals, or pass anything to the customers. Is that clear?' Bicker nodded.

As he reached for a pile of papers his nerves seemed to get the better of him and the papers scattered onto the desk. Bicker looked up; there was fear in his eyes. Amongst the papers Eddy could see a pamphlet with a title that made him stare at Bicker. The title was clear: Gay Liberation Front manifesto'. Bicker started to sweat and a whole host of emotions swept across his face. Eddy stared straight into Bicker's eyes and shook his head just enough for Bicker to see but not for Chris Stamford to notice. Bicker quickly gathered the papers and shoved them into a drawer in his desk.

As they made their way back to their car, they agreed that everything Bicker had told them was full of 'don't knows'. The most interesting piece of information he came out with was that the two men they wanted to know about would normally have been at the club the previous evening, but they had not turned up. Customers had actually asked for them and some got quite agitated when they found they were not on the premises. I think we both know what they were up to. Perhaps it would be a good idea to come back tonight to speak to a few of the customers.'

'Do that, and speak to as many as you can, not only the customers but the staff on the door and behind the bar.'

'Will you be coming?' Chris joked.

'You've got to be kidding. I'm the last sort of person you would see in a place like this, so no, ask Phil or Ray if they fancy a night of dance and romance.'

As they drove off, the radio crackled into life. It was Peter Russell. 'Delta two, this is Delta one, message, over.'

'Hello Delta two, send over.'

'I want you back at the office at 17:00 for a catch-up, over.'

'Rodger out.' Chris liked the way his boss was clear with his instructions and he knew that if he called a meeting it was clearly necessary.

13

Peter Russell had arrived back at his office to find a message on his desk to contact the Chief Superintendent's office as soon as he got in. He picked up the phone and dialled a four-digit number; the pleasant voice of Julia, the Chief Super's secretary answered. 'Ah, Inspector Russell, the Chief Superintendent would like to meet with you at 1pm tomorrow.'

There was no way that Peter could say no. 'Of course. Is that in his office?'

'Yes, and please bring any information you have regarding your current case.'

This puzzled him as he felt he had not gathered much intelligence so far. But if that's what he wanted, he was not going to argue.

At his 5pm meeting that day, Peter asked his team to run through what they had got so far. Chris Stamford stood up and went through the details of the club he and Eddy had visited, and also told Peter that Eddy and Phil would be going back that night to see what else they could dig up. It came as a surprise when the last DC of the squad told them of the frustrating news to do with Steyning's financial status and his banking arrangements. They had discovered that Steyning owned virtually nothing; the house was on a – very expensive – three-year lease, and anything of value was rented. His income stream was bizarre. Money from his clubs was paid into an English bank, the majority of the money then being transferred to an offshore bank account that was apparently based in Singapore. It was only running costs that remained in the UK account. That's as far as they had got. Peter Russell was pleased with the update from his team; they were solid and he knew he could rely on them.

'I seem to be the only one without much to show for my efforts today,' he said. This raised a few smiles, especially from Chris, who knew that his boss had been back to the hotel.

'I have asked the hotel to go back through their records and check to see if Steyning had used them at all, whether for accommodation or catering. They will let me know by tomorrow anything they discover.' Peter paused, then continued, 'There are a few things I would like you to follow up. Chris, if you could go back to the hotel and speak to the night staff. Concentrate on whether Steyning had met anyone in the hotel. And you two,' he motioned to Phil and Eddy, 'get as much as you can without resorting to drink and women. Ray, carry on digging re anything relating to the funding of Steyning's operation. Before you go, just to keep you in the picture, I have a meeting with the Chief Super tomorrow at 1 pm, so I need an update from you all before then if I am to retain his good opinion! Either come back here or ring me before 12.30. There was a scraping of chairs as the team got up and made their way out.

By 1 o'clock the following day, a file on Peter's desk contained all the latest information from the efforts of his team. He picked it up and made his way up the three floors to where the Chief Superintendent had his inner sanctum. As he knocked on the door, he was a rather worried as to why the Chief Super want to see him. He realised it was becoming a little more than just a case of a drug overdose, but he didn't think it warranted this sort of attention. The Chief Super's secretary met him at the door. She informed him with a smile that her boss was ready for him and asked him to take a seat. The intercom on her desk sounded and emitted a familiar voice that unfortunately seemed full of irritation. Just what he needed. He stood, straightened his tie and entered a large office that had all the prerequisites of someone in a position of power.

'Come in, Peter, and take a seat.' Sam Newham was a man with little time for pleasantries. As Peter entered, he saw a second figure, tall, with closely cropped, iron-grey hair and an expensive tan that matched his expensive suit. 'Peter, this is Commander Ian Bedford who wants to have a word with you about your current case.'

The Commander shook hands and suggested they go to his office. 'We will leave the Chief Superintendent to attend to far more important matters than mine.'

This did not sit easily with the Chief Super as he wanted to be in on what was going on, but Commander Bedford walked past Peter, opened the office door and ushered him through, calling out, 'Thanks, Sam,' as he closed the door.

Peter followed Ian Bedford as he made his way along various corridors until he reached his own domain. Although his rank was higher than Sam's, his office was more compact but had the benefit of a separate meeting room, which is where Peter found himself.

'This may seem a little strange to you, Peter, but bear with me. I'm sure you'll find it to your advantage.' Peter looked puzzled, but was curious. Ian Bedford opened the file Peter had brought with him and started to read. As he scrutinised it, he looked up from time to time but asked no questions. Once he had finished, he closed the file.

'That's pretty good considering you've only had the case for a very short time.'

'I have a good team working for me. They do the donkey work.'

'I don't believe it's only them for one moment. Let me explain who I am and what I would like you to help me with.'

Ian Bedford told Peter of his role, which was not within the Met, but was heading up a national unit that was being put together to combat serious and international crime, particularly drugs. He went on to describe how he envisaged his unit would function. Peter could not really see what this had to do with him until Bedford opened Peter's file again and stabbed his finger at Steyning's profile.

'The person you are investigating is of interest to me. He is known to my unit as being a serious player in the importation and distribution of drugs in this country. I know that the drug problem is not as big as, say, in America, but it is growing, and my job is to make sure it doesn't get out of control. I see by the forensic report that it was not heroin that killed Steyning but a new substance on the market. I have asked for help from our American colleagues to try to identify this new substance. This man Steyning had his fingers in a lot of pies and I need to know all about his contacts, suppliers, and users. I have no doubt whatsoever that he is responsible for supplying a great deal of the illegal drugs in the UK.

Peter looked surprised at the extent of Steyning's involvement.

'Peter, you have stumbled on the tip of an iceberg and I need to find out what's below the surface. I want you to carry on with your investigation, but report to me. Your team will remain the same, perhaps with an addition or two, but your squad will be centred on London and concentrate on the supply route of drugs entering the capital.

'What about the Chief Super, sir? I can't ignore his requests for updates on my investigation.'

'You leave Sam Newham to me, said the Commander. 'I assure you he will not bother you.' That remark surprised Peter and he said nothing as the Commander continued, 'You will be one of four squads, one here in London, one in Birmingham, one in Manchester and one in Newcastle. Although each squad will act independently, it will be necessary to coordinate certain lines of inquiry and action. With some carefully chosen assistants I will organise any national or international activity that is needed. Bedford could see the cogs in Peter's mind whirling. He waited a few minutes to let his points sink in.

'Coffee or tea?' Ian went to his intercom.

'Coffee, please, and could it be strong.'

'Two coffees, please, Margaret. And make them strong!'

The coffee arrived, brought in by a petite woman of about forty.

'Margaret, this is Peter Russell. You may be seeing a lot of him in the weeks to come.'

She held out her hand and as Peter stood to shake it, he felt a small but surprisingly firm hand. 'How do you do.' Her voice was very clear and her diction crisp. Placing the cups on the table she turned and left.

Ian watched her go. 'Don't be taken in by her diminutive stature,' he smiled. 'She is a vital part of my unit. Her powers of organisation put me to shame. Now, your thoughts, Peter.'

'It's a bit soon to say, but from what you have told me I think being involved in an operation like this is an opportunity I can't afford to miss. At the moment, though, I have so many questions buzzing around inside my head, I don't know where to start.'

'Fire away.' Bedford could almost smell his interest.

The questions flowed. Where would he and his team be based? What area would they be expected to cover? What sort of liaison would there be with local CID? Would he be involved in budgets? The questions flew thick and fast. Ian Bedford was impressed; there were more questions than he had expected. After what seemed like hours, he felt he had answered them all. Peter had a time frame and a reporting structure which he would brief his team on. His hope was that the team would be willing to join him on this journey.

Bedford concluded, 'I would like you to put all your efforts into tracing Steyning's organisation – by which I mean his clubs. The money chain, which I think will be our biggest challenge, links both London and elsewhere, and if that leads you to foreign parts, so be it. For the time being, leave the hotel alone. From the information on file, I don't think you'll benefit from spending any more time there.'

This last part did not please Peter, but he knew it was only because he wanted to develop a relationship with Annabel Stewart. Maybe in his own time he would book a table for dinner at the hotel.

'One last item.' Ian Bedford looked straight at Peter. 'I understand you have applied for two chief inspector vacancies in the last year, is that right?'

'Er, yes.' Peter was a little embarrassed by the question.

'Why didn't you get them?' A blunt question, but it would give him an indication of what Peter Russell thought were his weak points.

'In the first instance I suppose not enough experience. Some thought I might be too young, but at the age of thirty two I would not have been the youngest in the force. In the second instance ... er ... my face just didn't fit.'

Ian Bedford clasped his hands in front of him. 'My squad leaders are chief inspectors. Do you think you could carry out the role of chief inspector in my organisation?'

Peter answered without hesitation a straight yes.

'I will be in touch with you and anyone else who needs to be informed about your team's transfer to my command. Welcome to the unit, Peter.'

On that note the meeting ended.

*

At the Rosegarth things had returned to normal after the excitement of having the police investigating one of their customers. The kitchen was still busy preparing and serving up meals for guests of the hotel and the restaurant, and Ben's life had settled down into a sort of routine. It would always be slightly erratic, mainly because of his hours, but his life with Sophie and his aunt and uncle kept him on an even keel. His meetings with Sophie became even more difficult when she was accepted for a course at college, which left them still fewer opportunities to meet.

It was two months after the Steyning incident that David Burdett summoned Ben into his office. Ben had no idea why; he couldn't think of anything that had gone disastrously wrong. His job was going well and he got on with his fellow chefs.

'Come in, Ben, shut the door and take a seat.' Ben did as he was told, sitting opposite Burdett. He couldn't read Burdett's expression but it was a look of some concern without any humour to lighten it. Ben thought *this is going to be a telling off*, but he couldn't think for what.

'Have I done something wrong, Chef?'

A smile crept across Burdett's face. 'No, nothing wrong, Ben. I want to sound you out on a proposition that may do you the world of good.'

Ben became more attentive as curiosity built up inside him.

'I have had my counterpart in our sister hotel in Rheims on the phone to me regarding a possible exchange of commis chefs – someone who is almost ready to become a chef de partie.' Ben's ears pricked up. This sounded promising.

Burdett explained the situation to him. 'It would mean a commis chef from here exchanging places with another commis chef for at least nine months, if not a year. They would initially work as commis chef and then take on the role of chef de partie. The exchange would entail those selected to have some knowledge of each other's language and be prepared to be parted from family and friends for some time. The hotel would fund travel expenses, but once the individuals had reached their respective hotels it would be up to them to support themselves. Naturally they would be paid their salaries in the normal way. If the opportunity arose for them to earn extra at their hotels, then that would be perfectly acceptable. If either individual wanted to return home, for a holiday or just a visit, it would be at their own expense. The chef selected would be assessed on a monthly basis to ensure he was up to the job and that the hotel was not wasting its money.'

Ben's eyes were nearly out of their sockets. Wow, this could be the making of him. His mind was whirling at speed, so many thoughts sprang into his head. It was obvious to Burdett that this had really hit Ben full in the face and he seemed to be bursting with questions. When Burdett asked him what he thought, the dam burst and questions flew out nonstop. Finally, Burdett had to calm him down.

'I think your best bet would be to go home after your shift and discuss this with your uncle and aunt, Ben, and see what they think. It's a big decision and at the moment you can probably only see bright lights and opportunity, but once you've had time to discuss this with calmer people you may find that it's not all a bed of roses.'

The excitement surging through Ben's body made him feel light-headed and it took him a couple of minutes to catch his breath and regain his composure.

'When will this take place?'

'Slow down, Ben, it won't be for at least two months, so speak to your loved ones and let me know if you are up for the challenge. Give me an answer by next Wednesday and we can take it a step further. Remember, this is not just you. There will be another commis chef on the other side of the Channel going through the same emotions as you, and it depends on him wanting the same as you.'

14

Ben's mind was in a state of flux. He had never been abroad before, let alone lived in any country other than England. He would speak to his aunt and uncle and see what advice they could give him. And then of course there was Sophie. Sophie – what would he say to her? Could he leave her behind? He knew he couldn't take her with him. How long was he going to be away and could their friendship survive a separation?

When he had finished his shift, he tried to find Sophie, but there seemed to be a great deal of activity in reception and he could see her dashing around as she dealt with new arrivals. He tried to get her attention but failed. As he climbed onto his bike a fine mist of rain started to fall, but he was in such high spirits that a little bit of rain wasn't going to affect his mood. Pulling his waterproof around his shoulders he set off, thinking about what he would say to his aunt and uncle. How would they react? He hoped they would be pleased for him, but it was a big step to take. Putting his bike in the shed, he entered through the kitchen door.

'Anyone at home?' His call was not answered immediately and he called again, impatience getting the better of him. He could hear his aunt make her way down the stairs. 'Is Uncle Steve at home?'

Just as he spoke, his uncle's head appeared round the door. 'What's all the noise about?'

Ben was so pleased they were both in. 'Come and sit down, I've got something very important to discuss with you.'

His Aunt Sarah immediately thought it might be to do with his relationship with Sophie, possibly an engagement. She sat down at the kitchen table and watched Ben as he came towards her. She could see he was excited about something from the awkwardness of his movements. Ben waited for his uncle to sit and then started to tell them what David Burdett had discussed with him. After he had finished, there was a moment's silence.

'What do you think?' he asked.

'Ben, if it's what you want to do with your life, you know we will support you whatever you decide to do … as long as it's legal of course!' That was just like his uncle, to finish on a humorous note.

His aunt in the meantime looked apprehensive. 'It's a big step, going to another country, and you don't speak very much French. Will you get by with just pointing at things and hoping for the best?'

Ben grinned at his aunt. 'I can learn fast if I'm surrounded by French speakers. I'll have to, otherwise I won't survive!'

Their discussion lasted nearly two hours, until Steven said he had to get some sleep as he would be up early the following morning. But before he went to bed, he said to Ben, 'If you didn't go down that path it might be something you would regret for the rest of your life.'

As his uncle disappeared through the kitchen door his aunt put a hand on Ben's arm. 'What about Sophie? Have you spoken to her yet?'

'No, we're meeting tomorrow after she finishes her shift.'

'Are you coming here or are you going to her place?'

'I think it would be best if we went to her flat. She's

comfortable there and if she gets upset her dad will be there.'

His aunt's face looked grave. 'Don't you hurt that girl, she's the best thing that ever happened to you.'

'I'll try not to upset her – you know I wouldn't hurt her for the world, but she knows that I want to get on in life just as much as she does, and I'm sure she'll be on my side.'

It was not a good night for any of them. Ben just could not get to sleep. His thoughts kept on jumping from what it would be like in a French hotel to what reaction he would get from Sophie. He had a day off the next day and as he sat down to his breakfast his aunt appeared.

'Ben, if you decide to take up this offer there is an awful lot to think about. You don't even have a passport. What I want you to do is sit down and make a list of everything that's needed.'

His aunt was a great person for making lists. If there was ever anything to be done it needed a list. Each list she drew up was pinned onto her kitchen board, and when each item had been completed it was crossed off. Anything that needed special attention was circled in red. She was a born organiser. That was how Steven was able to concentrate on the practical aspects of his business. With his wife by his side, he knew that everything was under control. Ben agreed that he would make whatever list his aunt thought was required as long as she supervised it!

*

He met Sophie as she left the hotel.

'Hi, are we going to look at your lovely garden?' she asked. Ben took her hand. 'No, I thought we might go to your place. Do you mind?'

Sophie looked puzzled. 'Ok, are we going by tube or are you going to give me a ride on your cross bar?' she laughed, and Ben felt his enthusiasm drain from his body.

'Let's take the underground, it's safer than my bike.'

It wasn't a long tube ride and the stations passed very quickly. They were soon at Sophie's flat and discovered that her dad had not yet arrived home. Ben took Sophie into the front room and sat her down. Sophie was getting worried by this time and wondered what was he going to say.

'Sophie, something happened at work today that may mean a lot to me and to some extent to you. Mr Burdett has given me the opportunity of a lifetime and I need to talk to you about it because it's going to affect everyone I care about.'

Sophie was really alarmed now. 'Tell me, tell me, Ben, what's it all about?'

Ben sat very close to her and told her what had been suggested by David Burdett. Her initial reaction was mixed, so full of joy, and at the same time, sadness.

'Oh Ben, you've got to do it, it could mean so much and you might never get another chance like it.'

'But what about us?' Ben had thought Sophie would be the one to ask that question.

'Ben, if you care for me as much as I care for you, what's a little bit of water called the Channel going to do to us? I'm sure we will find a way to see each other and there is always pen and paper.' She looked up at him and he could see there were tears in her eyes. He felt rotten. Leaning forward he kissed her eyelids. She held him very tight and he could feel her body shaking as the tears flowed.

There was the sound of a key in the lock. Sophie pushed herself away from Ben. Her father came into the front room and he could see that his daughter had been crying. 'What going on?' he asked, frowning.

Sophie said that it was nothing and that Ben had had some

fantastic news about an offer from the hotel, and she explained to her dad what it was. He perched on the arm of the sofa and took his daughter's hand. She looked up with tears still in her eyes. He looked at Ben.

'It's a big step for you, Ben, but it's one that may only come your way once in a lifetime. I'm sure that Sophie and me don't want to see you go, but we both know you'll be back and when you do return you'll be all the better for it.' He didn't think he was making much sense and decided to get out of their way. 'If you want me, I'll be in the kitchen.'

Sophie's final words to Ben as he left were, 'Ben, please do what you want to do. We have the rest of our lives ahead of us and we will always be us, together, no matter if you're in France or Timbuctoo. We will always have each other.'

Ben had very mixed emotions as he made his way home. He admired how positive Sophie had been in her response, which made him feel very guilty. As he opened the front door, his aunt called out to him from the kitchen. She was still sitting at the kitchen table and in front of her was a sheet of paper that listed all the things that would need doing.

'No time like the present. How did Sophie take your news?'

Ben sighed. 'A lot better than I expected and a lot better than I deserve. I need to make sure she is in on whatever I do. She means so much to me and whatever I do in my life I want her to be a part of it.'

The next few days flew by. Ben found it difficult to concentrate and every spare moment he could find he spent with Sophie. They went over things that he would need and what he would have to do to make himself understood. Sophie bought him a French phrase book and an English-French dictionary. She seemed as excited as he was, but there were moments when he could see her thinking of the time they would be separated.

On the appointed Wednesday morning, Ben knocked on David Burdett's door and went in. Burdett looked up and smiled. 'Well, have you decided if you want to go for it?'

'Oh yes, I would really like to take you up on the offer.' There was a broad smile on his face but his stomach was churning; he had yet to get a firm offer, so he waited for his boss's response.

'Sit down, Ben. It's a massive step for you and it will take a lot for you to succeed in a foreign county, but I know you have the skill and enthusiasm that will see you through. Come back after your shift and we can really get into the nitty gritty.'

Ben left Burdett's office walking on air. His future seemed to be unfolding in front of him and he was a very happy individual.

After his shift he went back to Burdett's office. Burdett was on the phone, but as soon as he had finished he pointed to a chair and Ben sat down, eagerly awaiting what he was going to tell him. Burdett explained to Ben how the transfer would work. He would be under the head chef at the Hotel Durocort in the French city of Rheims. It was of the same high status as the Rosegarth and their kitchen was just as busy. Burdett had spoken to his counterpart at length and they had agreed that the exchange would be for an initial six months. That could be extended for a further six months if everything went well. There could also be an opportunity for Ben to stay even longer if all parties agreed and if it would be in the interest of both hotels.

'I have compiled a file giving you all the information you will need, and I strongly suggest you read it from cover to cover at least twice and then come back and see me. There are names you may not be familiar with and details you may have questions about. Don't be afraid to ask questions because you may not get another chance. Do you understand how important this is?'

Ben felt somewhat intimidated by the enormity of the undertaking as he took the file and headed for home. That night he settled down in his bedroom and started to read it. His attention was drawn to the details of the head chef, Craig Hinson, who was English by birth. He had married a French girl and had been living in France for the past twenty years. It went on to give a few details of his career, which impressed Ben. He also felt relief that hopefully he would not have to struggle with the language when talking to him.

Burdett had included a diagram of the French kitchen brigade structure, which was almost identical to the English one. He read that he would be employed initially as a commis chef and would shadow a member of the French brigade. He would be accommodated in the staff quarters of the hotel, a small single room with the use of a shower. That suited Ben, who did not envisage entertaining too many guests. Once the head chef was satisfied that Ben was equal to the job, he would be placed in the position of chef de partie, which is where he would get the majority of his training and experience. If the head chef thought it justified, he could be allowed to specialise in one of the stations in the kitchen.

He would be given a number of days' holiday when it would be permissible for him to travel home at his own expense. These days would be dependent on the demands of the hotel. He would be required to supply his own knives and any other implements he felt useful. The hotel would provide his uniform and the laundering. At the end of the file, a street map of Rheims had been provided with the hotel marked clearly.

As Ben read, he made copious notes and noted down other

questions. How would he get to Rheims? Who would he report to? Could he use a telephone in the hotel? What other details of the hotel were available – how many rooms, how large was the restaurant, how many covers – there was so much he needed to know.

The following morning at breakfast he looked up at his aunt's noticeboard on the kitchen wall, and sure enough there was the list detailing virtually everything he needed to do, every place he needed to visit, and how long he had to do all these things.

Hell, he thought, *that's an awful lot. Do I have enough time?* But he was determined that he would make enough time. Eight weeks, that's all he had, and he went at it full pelt. With the help of his aunt and Sophie he managed to fill in forms and buy a variety of essential items. Sophie helped him choose new clothes and shoes; she didn't want him looking anything but the smart Englishman when he arrived in France.

They eventually reached a point where they could do no more. He had his passport, and Sophie had also applied for one at the same time. 'You never know, I might pop over to see you,' she said, which pleased him and he hugged her.

His luggage was securely packed, tickets had been purchased and timetables studied. He would travel by train to Dover, cross to Calais, take the train to Paris where he would change from Gard Du Nord to Gard de l'Est, then hopefully go straight to Rheims. It should take him the best part of a day to reach the hotel and without much skill in French it was going to be quite tricky.

His days were mainly full of panic as one thing after another reared its head. Problems seemed to come from all directions, but with his family and Sophie's help he managed to overcome all the obstacles that came his way. The eight weeks disappeared in what seemed like the blink of an eye, and finally, thankfully, Ben felt he was ready to go, 'goodbye' and 'good luck' and 'lucky beggar' from his mates at the hotel ringing in his ears.

Ben would catch the train to Dover from Waterloo at eleven o'clock the following morning, so he went to say his goodbyes to Sophie. He knew this was going to be one of the hardest things he had ever had to do. He felt that leaving her in England would rip his heart out, but she had told him to go and get on with his life. They had made an agreement that they would speak on the phone at least once a fortnight and that before they parted they would buy each other a record that they could play when they thought of each other. Ben looked round his bedroom. He would be sad to say goodbye to his home. His aunt and uncle had been his world after the tragedy that his family had gone through. They had been his strength, offered him advice but let him make his own decisions.

Sophie was a different matter. His feelings for her were so great that he knew it would be gut-wrenching. He picked up the record he had bought for her, a Dusty Springfield LP that reminded him of the first time she had visited his home where they had played his uncle's record and fallen asleep listening to it.

As he walked towards Sophie's flat, he felt his emotions starting to run wild, but what could he do now? They had both agreed to the enterprise, he kept telling himself. He knocked on the door. Sophie was in her best outfit, her pink mini dress with the pink suede shoes. Her hair shone in the light in the hall and her face was a picture he would never forget. Sophie looked at him. He stood tall and straight; his fair hair was neat and his clean-shaven face looked smooth. She could see the green flecks in his eyes as he bent to kiss her. They held each other briefly. He took off his jacket to reveal a white shirt with button-down collar, and washed blue Levis. Ben kept the bag with the record in it for later, and they went into the front room.

It was a quiet evening. Sophie's dad had gone out and they had the flat to themselves. They sat for some time. Just being together was what they wanted. Sophie started by asking Ben if he had everything he needed. He replied that he could do with one more thing, but his suitcase wasn't big enough. They both laughed weakly – it didn't seem the time for laughter. They gave each other the records they had bought. Sophie gave Ben a Fleetwood Mac LP he had said he liked, and Ben handed over the Dusty Springfield record.

Ben blurted out, 'Will you wait for me, Sophie? I promise I will be back for you and we will be together for as long as you want me.'

Sophie couldn't hold back any longer. Her body shook with emotion and the tears started to fall. 'Of course I'll wait, you fool, who else am I going to get to cook for me?' It was now Ben's turn to show just how much she meant to him and he couldn't stop his own tears, his voice coming out as a choking rasp. They held each other so closely it was hard to pull apart when they heard the key turn in the front door.

Sophie's father came into the room and saw them on the sofa. 'I guess it's time for you to go, eh Ben?' He looked at his daughter's tear-stained face and his heart bled for her. Ben stood up slowly. Sophie held his hand tight and he gently pulled her to her feet. Sophie's dad held out his hand and Ben shook it warmly.

'You take care of yourself, lad, and remember you are one of us now and we want to see you back here whenever you can make it.'

'Thank you for your kindness, Derek. I shall be regularly in touch with Sophie by phone so we will be able to pass any news to each other.'

Still holding Sophie's hand, they made their way to the front door. Facing each other Sophie reached up and kissed Ben. It was her gentle kiss, her warm kiss, that was something he would carry with him on his journey. Sophie laid her head on his chest, not wanting to let him go but knowing she had to release him even though it felt like forever. Ben put on his jacket and reached for the door handle. Sophie clutched his arm as he opened the door. They kissed one last time, then Ben stepped outside. Sophie let go, she didn't want to, but she knew she had to.

The door closed. Ben looked at the door and knew that Sophie was on the other side. He could hear her crying. He reached out and as his fingers slid down the door, he could almost feel her.

'Are you alright, love?' The voice came from a woman walking along the corridor.

'Yes, yes, I'm ok,' Ben lied. The woman had jolted him back to reality, and slowly he made his way out of the building.

15

His journey home was not a pleasant one. His mood changed from elation to the lowest of the low. He kept on questioning himself whether he had done the right thing, whether he could really live without Sophie being by his side, and began to doubt he would be able to cope with the unknowns that lay ahead. It was a dismal night with a fine mist of rain soaking him without really trying. The rain just added to his misery. He approached the door to his house and felt dread that it would be a long time before he would walk up to the front door again. He didn't feel like talking, but his aunt caught him before he could escape up the stairs.

'Are you ok?' she asked, knowing it was a stupid question. The boy had just said goodbye to his girlfriend and who knows when he might see her again.

'I'm fine, I just feel tired and need to get some sleep.'

She could tell by his voice that he was just about all in. Everything that had happened over the last two months had taken its toll. Ben had been full of excitement one moment and at rock bottom the next. Still, she reasoned, at least he was entering a phase of his life that would soon fill his days and nights with something new and interesting.

'I'll see you at breakfast,' she said as she watched him head towards a restless night's sleep.

Steven had taken some time off to get Ben to Waterloo station in time for his train. He had discussed how he and his wife would say goodbye to him and decided that tears would not help matters, so Sarah would say farewell at home and Steve would see Ben into the station and say his goodbyes there. Breakfast seemed quieter than usual. Ben was occupied in thinking about the route he would be taking to reach Rheims, and his aunt and uncle just wanted to let him approach the day in his own way.

After the breakfast things had been tidied away, Ben went back to his bedroom and checked his suitcases, making sure they were properly closed and the small padlocks firmly fixed. It would be disastrous if he should lose anything before he arrived. He looked round, taking his time, at the familiar things that would disappear from his life, but – he told himself as he tried to cheer himself up – he must be positive; this was his chance to make something of himself. Lots of new experiences awaited him, in a different country, in a different hotel, and with a group of different colleagues. He picked up the two suitcases and heaved them down the stairs.

His uncle was waiting at the bottom. 'Time to go, Ben.' He opened the front door and took one of the suitcases. His aunt stood by the door. Ben could see her eyes glistening and he wondered to himself how many more women must he make cry. He put the suitcase down and hugged her.

She coughed and cleared her throat. 'You will phone and write, Ben, promise me you will.'

'Of course I will.'

'And you will speak to Sophie as often as you can?'

'I promise.' He gently pushed her away. 'Will you look after Sophie for me, let her visit and spend time in the garden?'

His aunt gazed at him tenderly. 'She can come here as often

as she likes and I promise you I will treat her like my own daughter.'

That was all Ben could ask for. Steven called from the car for Ben to get a move on.

Picking up the suitcase, Ben reached forward and kissed his aunt on the cheek. 'Take care of everyone,' he said.

She watched as the suitcases were loaded into the boot. Ben turned and waved as he got into the car. Sarah waved back until the car disappeared round a corner, then slowly closed the front door behind her.

Steven pulled into the Drop Off point at Waterloo station and helped Ben get his cases out of the boot. 'This is it,' he said as he straightened up. He held out his hand and as Ben took it he put his other arm around Ben's shoulders. 'Don't you start crying. I've had enough with Sophie and Aunt Sarah!' Steven looked at Ben; this young lad that had been living with him since he was a small boy, was leaving home for the first time. 'Come on or you'll miss you train.'

There was no risk of that, but Steven did not want to be hanging around for a long goodbye. They walked side by side, each with a suitcase, until Ben found a seat in the waiting area.

'What time's your train?'

'Oh, I've got at least thirty-five minutes yet.'

'Well, good luck, Ben, and take care of yourself. If anything were to happen to you, I would get one hell of a telling-off from your aunt.'

Ben smiled as his uncle turned and made his way out of the station. Ben followed his figure until he was lost in the crowd of tourists and workers milling around the station concourse. The train was on time and Ben made his way to the platform. A queue was starting to form, but the gates were opened just as he took his place, and people started to head towards the train. Ben looked up and down the platform and decided to aim for a carriage closer to the front of the train. He managed to get his cases up the steps and into the carriage, struggling to get them onto the luggage rack. He sat watching his fellow passengers pass by the window, others making their way between the seats, looking for a place to sit. He had chosen a seat with a table and took out a book he had brought with him entitled very simply, 'Rheims', which he thought would keep his mind occupied on the journey.

It wasn't long before a couple asked if the seats opposite Ben were free. Ben gestured that they were and the man lifted their cases onto the rack. As they seated themselves, Ben detected the scent of what could only be very expensive perfume. The woman was well dressed, and with her stylish makeup and hair she could have stepped out from a magazine cover. The man was equally smartly attired in a well-tailored suit and tie. The woman started to speak to her companion in French. Ben thought, *wow, my journey is already starting on a train in Waterloo station.*

Their conversation was brief while they made themselves as comfortable as they could. The woman looked at Ben's book and asked if Ben was on his way to France? Her English was very good and her accent made it sound somehow sexy.

'Er, yes.' There was no way he was going to try out his limited French and make a complete fool of himself.

'You are going to Rheims?' She pointed to his book.

'Yes.'

The conversation gradually started to flow – it was mainly the woman asking Ben questions, which he was happy to answer, and he slowly lost his shyness. She asked for the name of the hotel where he was going to work, and smiled when he told her it was the Durocort. Ben asked if she knew of the hotel and her companion said that they knew it very well and had visited it several times.

They introduced themselves as Charles and Theresa, and they had been in London to attend the launch of a new season's wine. It turned out they represented a champagne label from the region. Ben had never heard of it, but that was not surprising as he was really only familiar with the cheaper end of the market. They chatted over the next two hours, and Charles suggested that Ben might find it easier if he were to follow them as the journey could be a little confusing, especially changing trains in Paris. Ben sighed with relief and told them he would be forever in their debt. It seemed they lived to the south-east of Rheims in a town by the name of Épernay in the champagne region of France. Theresa described the area to Ben, who visualised the rolling vineyards under sunlight skies; it seemed very enticing. He could not believe his luck as he followed the couple from train to boat and boat to train.

The ferry was another first for Ben. They made their way into the passenger lounge and pushed their baggage safely under their seats. The ship started to rumble, in preparation for leaving; *a sort of maritime indigestion,* Ben thought. The movement of the ship didn't seem to bother him as he had supposed it might. Theresa touched Ben's arm and pointed out of the window, or should that be porthole? Ben followed her arm and could see Dover and its famous white cliffs starting to recede. *This is it,* he thought, *no going back now, I'm totally committed.*

He began to feel weary, and as he sat back on the bench seat, his eyes slowly closed. He woke with a start to the sound of the engines making a strange noise and the ferry slowing down. As he looked up, he saw Charles sipping a cup of coffee and he told Ben they had arrived in Calais. French soil. Ben looked at Charles and Theresa and wondered how he would have managed without them. At Passport Control he got out his brand-new passport and work permit and had them scrutinised by a very officious French officer.

'What is the purpose of your visit to France?' he demanded. *Not a great deal of Gallic charm here,* Ben thought. 'I've come to work at the Hotel Durocort in Rheims.'

'And what will you be doing at the Hotel Durocort?'

'I'm a chef and I shall be working in their kitchen.'

His work permit was checked and handed back with his passport. The official muttered something under his breath that Ben could not make out, and a thump of the stamp on a clean page of his passport told Ben he was through. He had lost sight of Charles and Theresa, but after a few minutes' panic he spotted them waiting for him,

'Bloody hell, I must keep my eyes peeled,' he said to himself. 'I don't want to lose them.'

The train ride to Paris was uneventful. Ben watched the passing countryside and the various towns they passed through. Different styles of houses with similar gardens backing onto the railway, grimy towns leading to open green fields and farmland. When they entered the crowded Gard du Nord, Ben was determined not to let Charles and Theresa get more than six feet away from him! They successfully made their way through Paris and boarded the train for Rheims at the Gard de l'Est.

When they pulled into the main station at Rheims, Ben already knew that his new friends would be continuing for another hour or so until they reached Épernay. He was curious to know why they took the train when they clearly appeared to be wealthy enough to fly, and he ventured to ask. Theresa told him her husband didn't like flying and if they could avoid it they did, and anyway they had more time on a train and a chance to meet interesting people. This made Ben blush slightly, at which Theresa smiled. After a bit of a struggle, Ben got his suitcases down from the rack and saying his goodbyes, left the train. Standing on the platform of Rheims Central Station he was finally on his own. He knew he had enough francs in his wallet to get a taxi and to last him until he got sorted out. Taking a deep breath, he headed for a taxi and his new life.

The taxi driver eventually roused himself from his boredom to make an effort at understanding Ben's poor pronunciation, and headed for the Durocort. Ben looked out of the window and was fascinated by the architecture of the city. They passed an impressive Gothic structure which he thought must be the cathedral. The driver brought the car to a halt in front of an imposing building with a revolving door that presumably led to the foyer. Ben paid the taxi driver after some discussion about price which Ben did not fully understand, but he thought he did ok. He didn't know which entrance to use, or whether there was a staff or tradesman's side door. He took the bull by the horns and went through the revolving door and into reception. The staff behind the desk watched him approach. Ben nervously tried his basic French.

'Je m'appelle Ben Croxley.'

The girl and the man behind the desk looked at each other and said simultaneously, 'English.'

'Yes.' Ben's confidence suddenly deserted him and any French he had taught himself went out of the window. He looked and felt hopeless. The girl behind the desk seemed to take pity on him and said with a fairly good English accent, 'Can I help you?'

Relief flooded over Ben. 'Yes, please, if you would. I'm here to see Monsieur Hinson.'

The girl looked at Ben's cases and picked up the phone. Ben could only make out a few words as the exchange was too fast for him, and a sudden sense of homesickness fell over him.

'Chef will be here soon.'

Not the friendliest of receptionists, he thought, but he was grateful for her help. Down the hallway came two figures – a tall man in chef's whites, clearly in control, and a younger man also in chef's whites.

'Ben, hi.' The tall man held out his hand, which Ben eagerly shook. 'I'm Craig Hinson.' He was about forty-five with grey hair and a face that had seen some trying times. 'Welcome to the Durocort. I expect you're worn out after your journey?'

Ben thanked every lucky star that he was now in the hands of somebody he could understand.

'I'm just pleased I managed to get here in one piece.'

'This is Georges. He will be your mentor until you have found your feet and I am satisfied with your work.'

Georges, almost as tall as Ben, with an olive complexion and very black hair, held out his hand, and Ben shook it firmly.

'Bonjour, Ben.'

That was to be the start of a period of Ben's life that would give him a great deal of pleasure despite an underlying mixture of nervousness and dread in case he didn't come up to scratch. The days and weeks that followed certainly proved taxing. He learnt the language of the kitchen from Georges, who was very patient with him. Ben discovered he was from Marseilles and had been with the Durocort for four years. Basically, for the first three weeks, Ben just listened and learned. He gained a certain amount of respect when the rest of the staff saw him in action, as he was soon able to demonstrate a decent skill level, right through from preparation to taking his dishes to the pass. He worked hard and it was tiring. He would collapse in his room at the top of the hotel and try to sleep. He had made a phone call to let everyone know he had arrived safely and had a further call when he got the chance to speak to Sophie. Georges helped him a great deal, his sharp tongue keeping Ben up to the mark, and Ben soon became more familiar with the terms used in the kitchen. He had a weekly chat with Craig Hinson at which he would assess his progress.

'You're doing better than I expected, Ben, but you have a long way to go.' Hinson stamped down early on in training so as not to let young chefs think too much of themselves. Ben was determined to improve and insisted that Georges always tell him when he went wrong. The methods used in the kitchen differed from those at the Rosegarth, and the sauces were more complex, but he put his head down and gathered more knowledge and skill by the day. He formed a working friendship with Georges, who kept telling Ben that he would never be understood unless he learnt to speak French properly. He tried to get Ben to speak with a French accent rather than an English one, but Ben found it hard to roll his r's and created a great deal of amusement in the kitchen when he did.

16

Life continued at a pace and Ben settled down into his role. He had little time to himself as when he was not working, he was sleeping. Georges invite him out for a drink, which Ben agreed to, but halfway through the evening his head was on his chest, so it did not immediately lead to other invitations.

Sophie kept up a regular flow of letters and whenever he got the chance, he would speak to her on the phone. His heart leapt when he heard her voice and they could have talked for ages had they not been so conscious of the fact that the phone calls were not cheap.

After he had been in France for two months, Craig Hinson invited Ben to his house for lunch, which Ben knew was not going to be a pie and a pint. He knew that when the French had lunch it was a two- possibly three-hour event. When it was in someone's home it would mean all the family came, especially on a warm day when they could lunch outside.

Ben dutifully made his way to his boss's house, which he had been to on a previous occasion to deliver some bits and pieces for the chef's wife. It was a surprisingly modern house, not what one would expect in an area so steeped in history. Built in the 1960s it had a slightly stark appearance on account of its very angular design. The colour of the facing brickwork helped it blend in to a degree, but Ben thought it lacked something as it clashed with the elegant buildings along the same road.

Craig Hinson's wife met Ben at the door. She was a very petite woman with the longest eyelashes he'd ever seen, which gave her, he thought, something of a Romany appearance. Her tanned face had a bewitching smile that caught Ben short when she greeted him. He remembered her name, but found 'Aglae' hard to pronounce, and when he tried, it brought a smile to her face as he stumbled over the pronunciation. She showed Ben through the house into the garden where his boss and his children were seated round a large table covered in a wonderful tablecloth of light blue that shimmered in the sunlight.

'Ben, come and sit down.' Craig pulled out a chair for him. 'You've met my wife, so now let me introduce you to my children.' Three young girls were sitting along one side of the table. 'This is Veronique, this is Michelle, and this is my youngest, Angelique.'

The girls were aged between eight and twelve and were full of giggles. They had their mother's colouring but a slender shape that was probably a mix of both mother and father. He said hello to each of them and they responded in quite fluent English. Craig said Ben would not be able to hide from them as all three were dying to practise their English on him.

Craig served the meal and it was everything Ben expected; a first course of mixed salad together with some charcuterie which tasted as delicious as it looked. As they were eating, one of the girls asked Ben if he had eaten grenouilles, and to their surprise he said he had. He had tried them early on in his time at the hotel and found them delicious. In fact he had tried them together with escargot, but had preferred the frogs – snails didn't do anything for him.

The talk at the table turned to how long Ben had spent in

Rheims and how he was managing. When he told them it was a very beautiful city, they warmed to him and all started talking at once. 'I have to be honest, though,' he said, and explained he had not yet had enough time to see everything he would like to.

'You must be due for some time off,' Hinson said. 'Perhaps it would give you chance to get to know the city better.' But Ben had other ideas for any time off he was owed. He said a little apologetically that he really would like to get a short break to England and that he had enough saved for a return ticket. Hinson asked when he was thinking of going and Ben replied that of course he would fit in with any staff needs the hotel might have. Hinson thought for a moment. 'I think we could spare you for a week at the end of next month. That would be after your first three months is up. How would that suit you?'

Ben wasn't expecting that and he almost choked on his food.

'If I could take a week off then, I'd be very grateful.' He felt his response was a little deferential, but if that's what it took to get him home for a week, so be it. Hinson said to leave it with him and he would see what he could do.

Ben left the Hinson house full of expectation; he could be going home at the end of next month! He would have to phone home and let everyone know. The following day, a Sunday, meant that Sophie would be with his aunt and uncle. He dialled home and felt a surge of excitement as his uncle answered. After getting the pleasantries over with, Sophie came on the line.

'Sophie, you'll never guess what – I'm due some holiday and can get home for a week at the end of next month.' There was a scream at the other end of the line and Ben could hear Sophie telling his aunt that he was coming home. Ben had to calm her down and get her to tell his aunt it would only be for a week To Sophie it didn't matter how long or how little – he was coming home and she would see him in the flesh. The phone was passed from Sophie to his aunt then to his uncle and then back to Sophie.

'Is it definite that you can get home?' she asked excitedly.

'There shouldn't be a problem and of course I'll let you know if anything comes up that might stop me.'

'Oh Ben, it will be so good to see you. I can't wait.' The conversation ended with love being passed back and forth. Ben hung up the receiver and punched the air. He felt good.

The next hours and days passed slowly although the kitchen was busier than ever, Visitors and restaurant guests just seem to multiply for no apparent reason. He realised it was all good business and the more time he spent improving his skills, the better. He had packed the smaller of his two suitcases and made sure he remembered the small gifts he had managed to get from the Boulingrin covered market held on a Saturday, and one or two bits from the art deco area. He was ready.

Saying 'à bientôt' to Georges was easy as they both knew he would be back in a week. Ben asked Georges if he could do him a big favour while he was away and try to find a 'tourne-disque' (a record player), for him. So far he had been unsuccessful in buying one. It took a bit of looking at the dictionary and a lot of comic hand movements to make sure Georges knew what Ben wanted. Ben also made it as clear as he could that it had to be 'bon marché'. Georges could only smile at Ben and nod as a sign of understanding.

The journey back to London was no way as terrifying as his outward trip. He still had a worry about negotiating his way from one Paris station to another, but he managed without difficulty, and once he got to Calais he relaxed. The ferry crossing was choppy but not enough to upset his stomach. He noticed others heading for the various toilets and tried to avoid them. He reckoned they would be in a pretty sorry state by the time they were three-quarters of the way across the Channel.

He went up on deck and watched the white cliffs come into view. Not long now! He suddenly realised that he was finding it strange to hear English spoken all around him as he had become accustomed to listening intently to French conversation and then trying to translate it into English in his head. By the time he was standing on the platform of Dover Priory station he felt more acclimatised and comfortable.

Ben had a sense of home when the outskirts of London came into view. They might be grey and grimy but he was home. The Kinks song 'Waterloo Sunset' must come into everyone's mind as they approached the station, he thought; it was just one of those songs and he could hear the lyrics in his head.

As long as I gaze on Waterloo sunset I am in paradise.

Public transport was not for him this time. He went to the first taxi that he saw and jumped into the back with his suitcase.

'Where to?'

Ben gave him his address and off they went. The buildings engulfed the cab as it weaved its way through the London traffic. He had been travelling all day and was tired and hungry, but that did not dampen his excitement as the cab drew up outside his house; he thought of it as his house because it was home.

The street lights were just coming on as he knocked on the door. There was some noise and what he thought were giggles behind the door before it opened. Sophie was in front and flew at him, nearly knocking him back down the steps. Her kiss took his breath away as she forgot everything and everyone and entwined herself round him. His aunt and uncle stood back and just laughed.

'Put him down, Sophie, give him chance to get inside,'

Steven joked, and she reluctantly disentangled herself.

As he entered, the smell of home hit him. How he had missed that special aroma that came from his aunt's cooking, her flowers and furniture polish. He dropped his case and they all went into the front room. Sophie had linked arms with Ben and was not letting go. When they had settled and tea with biscuits had been laid out in the front room, Aunt Sarah asked the dreaded question. 'When do you have to go back, Ben?' The three of them looked at him, not really wanting to hear the answer.

'In seven days, and I've already lost a day in travelling so I intend to make every second count!'

Sophie looked at Ben and told him that every one of those seconds would include her, whether he liked it or not. This caused some light laughter but underneath, sadness took their feelings to another place.

'I have to drop a letter off to Mr Burdett at some point. It's from the head chef at the Durocort, so I guess it's some sort of report to let him know if the exchange is working. Other than that, I am free as a bird.'

Sophie and Sarah looked at one another and something passed between them, unspoken but fully understood.

His aunt said, 'We have a few ideas, Ben, but perhaps that can wait till tomorrow after you've had some rest.'

Ben did feel shattered. His eyelids were drooping and he had difficulty in stopping his head from dropping to his chest. His uncle suggested some good old fish and chips might help to keep Ben awake, and made to leave the room. As he reached the door, he asked what they would like; the response was unanimous – 'Cod and chips!' He smiled and left the room. Sarah cleared the tea things away and asked if they would prefer eating in the dining room or the kitchen. They replied in unison: 'Kitchen!'

His aunt left them and Ben looked at Sophie. Although tired he thought to himself, *how did I manage to get a girl as beautiful as her? God, I really love her.* Sophie reached up and kissed him again, this time affectionately on the cheek.

'Your aunt has said I can stay the night – in the spare room of course.'

She blushed, and Ben grinned. 'No hanky panky, then.'

'Definitely not,' she replied humorously.

The food came and was eaten between questions being fired at Ben. He answered the best he could between mouthfuls, but as they finished, he said he needed to unpack and get sorted out. He made his way to his bedroom carrying his case and was overjoyed to see his familiar things and that everything was still as it was when he left. Putting his case on the bed he began to unpack. The presents he had brought could wait until the morning when he would feel refreshed. He checked his watch. It was nearly half past eleven and he'd been on the go all day. There was a light knock on the door and Ben saw Sophie appear, smiling at him.

'Just to say good night and don't you dare do anything without me.'

Ben looked at her and was glad to be home. 'I won't. I promise.' She came into the room, crossed to his bed and kissed him.

'Goodnight, Ben, love you.'

''Night, Sophie, love you too.'

The following day set in motion a whirlwind of activity. Sophie and his aunt had made plans and he had no choice but to follow where they led him. Shops and lunches, walks and talks – the time seemed to fly. As they walked down the high street they stopped in front of Woolworth's.

'What about some 'Pic'n Mix?' Sophie tugged on Ben's arm and almost dragged him into the shop. She got her sweets and as they headed towards the doors Ben saw the photo booth. 'C'mon, Sophie, let's get some photos.'

Sophie looked in the small mirror and made sure her hair was not a mess, pulled back the short curtain and sat on the stool.

'I'm a bit too high.'

'Swivel it round.' Ben made a turning motion with his arm.

When Sophie decided she was at the right height, Ben put in the necessary coins and a few seconds later there was a flash. A quick changeover and it was Ben's turn to sit on the stool, which he quickly adjusted. Flash! His image was captured. The next flash took place as Ben was pulling Sophie into the booth so that they could get a photo of them both together. As fast as they could, they arranged themselves in front of the camera and looked into the screen. Flash! They were done.

After waiting for what seemed an age, a strip of photos fell from the innards of the machine. Sophie grabbed them and started to laugh as she held them up to Ben. He saw a startled Sophie, him looking like a terrorist, a blurred vision of the two of them half out of the booth, and one nice one of the two of them. He joined Sophie in her laughter. When they reached home, they cut the photos up neatly and threw the blurred ones away. Ben put the picture of Sophie in his wallet and Sophie carefully placed Ben's picture into her purse.

17

On the third day Ben told Sophie that he must go to the hotel to see Burdett. He knew Sophie didn't want to go to her place of work while he was on holiday, but needs must. They arrived at the Rosegarth and found Sophie's boss behind the reception desk; she looked surprised to see them. 'I thought you were off? You don't seem to able to keep away, the pair of you.'

She asked Ben how things were going and what his plans were. He replied he was about to see his boss and hopefully would have some idea of what lay ahead. She wished him luck and they headed towards the kitchen. As they walked, Sophie asked Ben if he wanted to hear a bit of gossip.

'Mm, always interested in gossip,' Ben grinned. 'Go on, what have you heard?'

Sophie looked around. 'It's not what I've heard but what I've seen.'

Ben was even more interested. 'Sophie what is it? 'Don't keep me in suspense.'

She lowered her voice as if she was about to spill some state secret. 'Well, I've seen my boss with that detective who interviewed you – you know, the one who asked about the outside catering you did where the man was killed.'

'That's an interesting combination – Inspector Russell and Annabel. Has it been going on very long?'

'I think they may have had one or two meals in the restaurant, but no more than that.'

'That doesn't mean they're having a passionate affair.'

Sophie pulled Ben back slightly and said, 'They've also been seen together away from the hotel. One of the bell boys saw them on the tube together.'

Ben snorted. 'It still doesn't mean they've been doing anything that might get them into trouble.'

'Well, I just thought I should keep you up to date with the goings on in the hotel!'

Ben looked for Burdett but couldn't see him. He was not in his office but in the main kitchen, explaining something to a face that was new to Ben.

'Ah, Ben, come and meet your opposite number. This is Claud, a very fine chef.'

Claud didn't really know how to take that. He held out his hand, embarrassed, and greeted Ben in English.'

Ben responded in French.

'We really are getting very cosmopolitan, aren't we?' said Burdett with a laugh. Ben followed him into his office.

'I have a letter for you from Mr Hinson,' Ben said.

'Right, let's see how he thinks you're doing, shall we?'

Sophie held Ben's hand as they waited for Burdett to comment on the letter. Burdett finished reading it and looked up.

'Well, it seems you've made a good impression, Ben. It's good to know you have proved that English chefs are just as good as home-grown French ones. Is there anything you need from me?'

Ben was very pleased and squeezed Sophie's hand. 'Not that I can think of. Just to say thanks for giving me such a great opportunity.'

Burdett looked serious. 'Remember you have only just started, there's a lot more to be done yet. I don't think another week's holiday will be coming your way for some time, so keep your plans flexible. As for you, young lady, no trying to entice him back here before he's accomplished what he set out to do!'

Sophie was surprised that Ben might not get another chance to get home in the near future.

Burdett looked at her kindly. 'Perhaps you might be able to go to France to see him? You never know what might turn up.'

Sophie had not thought of that, but the seeds had been sown.

They had a hectic time going from shop to shop, which was more for Sophie's benefit than Ben's, although he did get Sophie to go with him to Soho, but only to Foyles Bookstore. Ben had decided to try and read French, even though he could still speak very little. He bought a book by Georges Simenon, a Maigret novel called 'A night at the Crossroads', and a pocket French/English dictionary, the reverse of the one Sophie had bought him to go with. His idea was that he would try to work his way through the novel while he was travelling and continue with it when he got back to the Durocort.

All too soon the time came for him to pack his suitcase again. Sophie was the most difficult to say goodbye to. They had had a great time just being together. Ben knew she would not let go easily so he tried to smooth the way for her. He managed to get a table at a French restaurant and using his basic French, tried to make it an evening to be remembered. It went well, but the tears still flowed as Ben left the house. Ben, hoping to make it a bit easier for her, reminded her what David Burdett had said, that she could always go to France to see him. This didn't cut much ice, she said. 'How could I do that when I have never been abroad before. I would be scared going to a foreign country on my own.'

They were still speaking about it when they got back to Ben's house. Being curious, aunt Sarah heard the conversation and poked her head round the door.

'Sophie, if you looking for someone to go to France with, I'm sure I could take a few days off and go with you.' That was just what Ben needed to hear. He saw Sophie's eyes light up and her mood instantly change.

'Would you really?' Sarah went over and put a hand on Sophie's shoulder. 'It would do me and Steven a great deal of good to get away from each other for a few days, or even a couple of weeks!'

'There you are, Sophie,' Ben grinned. 'Things aren't so bad after all. It would be fantastic if you could get to France with Aunt Sarah.'

Ben took Sophie home. He knew she had to be at work the following day and that he would have to say his farewells that night. Even though Ben's aunt had cheered her up, she still had difficulty in saying goodbye. As Ben heard the door lock click behind him, he wondered how long it would be before they saw each other again. That was in the lap of the gods.

Steven drove Ben to the station. 'It's been good having you back, but your aunt and I know that you have your dreams and that you must follow them.'

'Thanks, Uncle Steven. Will you carry on looking after Sophie for me? She thinks she's stronger than she is and might need some of your steadying influence to keep her in touch with reality.'

'I'll do my best,' he said, shaking Ben's hand. 'Good luck and keep safe.'

The journey back to France took on a familiar aspect as Ben settled down to try to read his Maigret novel and watch the Kent countryside pass by his window. He found no real need to get into conversation with any other passengers so it was an uneventful trip. It was only when he reached Paris that he felt he had returned to France, when the smell of Gitanes, Disque Bleu and Gauloise, hit him. As he walked past the cafés, what also struck him was how people were happy to sit outside on the pavement, watching the world go by. He thought that going from eggs and bacon back to coffee and croissant would be something a little hard to take, but he reminded himself that this was where his life was and that he had better make the most of it.

At the Durocort he was welcomed back by Georges who, in broken English, said that he had 'un cadeau', a gift for him. Ben went to his room and Georges left him, returning rapidly with a large box under his arm. Ben's curiosity got the better of him.

'Qu'est ce que c'est?'

Georges put the box down and began to unwrap 'un tourne-disque'. Ben couldn't believe his eyes. Wherever had he found it? He clapped his hands on Georges' shoulders. 'Thank you – merci, Georges. Combien?'

Eventually Ben discovered the price, both of doing their best to make it easy for the other to understand. The price was nicely within his means. He tried to ask Georges where he bought it, but could not get a reply he could understand. He plugged the record player in and switched it on. He opened the larger of his two suitcases and from beneath several layers of clothing pulled out the Fleetwood Mac LP that Sophie had given him. Carefully he removed the record from its sleeve and placed it on the turntable, gently lowering the needle until it came into contact with the vinyl. The first track 'Need Your Love so Bad' nearly knocked him over.

'Merci,' he said again.

'À plus tard.' Georges gave a shrug and left him to it.

'À demain, Georges.'

He listened to the end of the LP and went to sleep feeling sad and happy at the same time.

Georges and Ben did not normally spend a great deal of time in each other's company outside of the kitchen. They saw enough of each other when they were working. That day they shared an annoying and frustrating shift when two customers sent their food back because it was too spicy for them. Neither Ben nor Georges could understand why they had ordered something that was clearly marked on the menu as being from the Middle East with a range of flavours including cumin, coriander and chilli. 'The customer is always right' being standard kitchen philosophy, they accepted the complaint as a part of their learning curve.

This incident led Georges to ask Ben if he would like to get a drink in the city. They both had the following day off, so Ben readily agreed. They headed towards the city centre and decided on a small café in one of the less central streets. Ben ordered a beer. Georges said he would have a 'citron presse' as he didn't drink alcohol, which surprised Ben as not too many chefs could say the same.

They sat and talked about the day, its ups and downs, and agreed it could have been worse and tomorrow was another day. Ben didn't know a great deal about Georges and asked him if he missed Marseilles. His immediate response was that Rheims was his home.

'Don't you have family? Ben asked.

'I have a brother who lives in Paris. He moved there when I secured the job here.'

The conversation took time as they both stuttered and stalled when trying to explain what they meant.

'What about Marseilles?' Ben asked. 'What is it like?'

Georges looked at Ben and shook his head. 'Marseilles has good places and some very bad places.'

'What made you leave?'

Georges studied his glass for a moment and then started to tell Ben about his life before Rheims. The way Georges told his story suggested a lot of hidden pain. His description of not being able to remember his parents and how his brother had looked after him was traumatic to say the least. His brother could do anything, according to Georges. He had looked after him, made sure he was well fed and that he got to school – well, most of the time. He went on to say that in Marseilles there were gangs dealing in anything that had a value, and unfortunately his brother was part of that scene. Georges had to finish with school so as to get a job and pay his way; his brother could only do so much.

'What is your brother called?'

'Oh, his name is Theo.'

After taking a sip of his drink, Georges continued with his story, telling Ben that things became very risky for his brother. Apparently, he had tried to get some people from North Africa into France and it had gone wrong. The people he was involved with did not care about the individuals trying to enter the country, and when they were abandoned by the boat that was towing their skimpy craft, Theo managed somehow to get them safely to the shore. Through other contacts, Theo got them to Paris and into a community where they would not be discovered easily. The gang concerned labelled Theo a thief for taking their property and their profit. This was not good for Theo; life was not considered of much value in that quarter of Marseilles.

Theo had got Georges a job washing dishes in a respectable small restaurant. Georges worked hard and the chef there had taken him under his wing. This gave him a modicum of protection, but best of all gave him time to learn catering skills.

The chef who Georges worked for was a former baker, and the first thing Georges learnt was how to make croissants, which he did day after day until his chef considered there was nothing to improve on. He went on to help make the many varieties of pastries sold by his employer. By the time Theo told Georges they would have to leave, he had become a pretty good patisserie chef in his own right.

Theo managed to get Georges an interview at the Durocort for a position as escuelerie, and that's where his relationship with the hotel had started. Ben asked if he ever saw his brother.

'I see him when I go to Paris, which is not very often. He is still dealing with some dangerous people.'

Georges told Ben that his brother had to learn how to defend himself and had tried to teach Georges. It was mainly how to use a knife, the main weapon used by the street gangs of Marseilles, but Georges was not very good with a knife and the thought of stabbing or even killing someone did not sit well with him. His brother, though, was a different story; he had been in many fights and had become well versed in the use of a very sharp switchblade knife.

'Why knives, why not guns?' Ben had very little idea of what he was talking about. Just the thought of gang warfare brought a scene from a film to mind where guns were used, but his only experience was movies.

'Guns are expensive. They make a lot of noise and most importantly they can be traced.'

Georges looked very grim. 'Knives are the favoured weapon

in the darker areas of Marseilles. If you ever meet my brother, be careful to make sure he gets to like you because he is the sort of person you do not want as an enemy.'

Ben took out his wallet to pay and Georges noticed the photo of Sophie. 'Is that your girl?' he asked curiously. Ben carefully extracted the photo and passed it to Georges.

'Très jolie.'

'Oui, très jolie.'

'Next time we come to a café I shall bring *my* girl for you to meet,' Georges replied.

'That would be very good.'

Their evening over, Ben felt he knew Georges a lot better and regarded him in a different light.

18

In the kitchen things were going well. Ben had been moved around several different stations to learn a variety of skills; one he particularly enjoyed was the sauté chef or saucier. He really felt able to be creative, but at the same time knew that if he got it wrong, the dish would be ruined.

As regards other aspects of life in the kitchen, it gradually dawned on him that one of the waitresses had been standing a lot closer to him than was comfortable. She was an attractive curvy thirty-year-old by the name of Gabrielle. She would smile and move near whenever she could, but her attention to him made him nervous. Ben didn't really know how to handle her so he tried to be merely pleasant, which turned out to be the wrong move. It seemed as if she was encouraged by his response and got even closer to him.

He watched her as she moved from kitchen to dining room. She was a very well-shaped woman, her grey pencil-skirt showing off her figure to its best advantage, and when she walked, Ben guessed she knew what men would be thinking. Georges had noticed what was going on and at the end of service called Ben to the window that overlooked the car park.

'Look, Ben.'

Ben could see Gabrielle walking towards a car. As the door opened, a man of about six-foot-four uncoiled himself. Gabrielle reached up and kissed him before they both got into the car and drove off.

Georges looked at Ben. 'Son mari – how is in English?' He pointed to his ring finger.

Ben realised what he was trying to say. 'Her husband?'

'Yes,' Georges said, 'that's right, her husband.' He picked up a rather long carrot, held it in front of Ben and snapped it in two. 'Il est très jaloux.'

After being put right by Georges, Ben avoided Gabrielle like the plague, not going anywhere near her, and if he saw her approaching he would find somewhere to disappear to. Fortunately, it seemed to work. She became bored trying to chase him and turned her attention to one of the young commis chefs. Ben realised he had had a narrow escape from the clutches of Gabrielle.

He concentrated on his work, practising one sauce after another, from basic aioli to a more complex Café de Paris. The important thing was that he enjoyed what he was doing and as long as the head chef was happy, so was he.

A week after he had managed to get Gabrielle off his back, Georges asked if he wanted to go to the café again and that this time he would introduce Ben to his girlfriend. It was just what Ben could do with. It had been some time since his trip home and the days were getting shorter as the winter season drew on. The weekly phone calls kept him in touch with Sophie, but speaking on the phone lacked so much, and although he had such a lot to say he seemed to forget it when the time came to speak.

It came as a bit of a surprise to Ben when he entered the café and saw Georges sitting with a rather beautiful girl. She sat straight-backed, and as Ben approached, she looked up with the most gorgeous almond eyes. Her complexion was that of light honey and just as smooth. As she opened her mouth to speak, Ben could see bright white even teeth. Georges stood, and with a sort of formal nod of the head said, 'Permettez que je présente Odette.' Ben thought she blushed slightly, but he could have been wrong. He held out his hand and thought hard how to respond in French. He took a breath and said, 'Heureux de faire votre connaissance.' He didn't know if that was right but he thought it came out ok.

Odette smiled and said in precise English, 'Oh, you speak French.' Ben was relieved and replied that he spoke a little not very good French and his English was certainly better.

Odette smiled and turned to Georges. 'Shall we speak in English today, so that we can practise?'

Georges looked uncertain – her command of English was far better than his. 'Ok, but speak slowly and stop when I ask.' He ordered some coffees and they settled down. Ben was impressed to hear that Odette was studying languages at the university. *'Wow, intelligent as well as beautiful, she is quite some catch,'* he thought. She was easy to talk to and she made sure Georges felt part of the conversation, carefully translating anything he didn't understand.

Ben thought that she possessed a skill with words and would make a brilliant teacher. He was curious as to how and when Odette came to be in Rheims. It transpired that her father was French and her mother Egyptian and that they had met in Cairo when her father was part of a delegation to the Egyptian government. They had fallen in love, and after marrying moved to her father's home city of Rheims. She had been born with a love of words and knew from an early age that languages were what she wanted to be involved with. She told him that she wanted to study the source of language, its origins, and how it had devcloped into what it was today. Ben thought that was a little deep for him so he asked which languages interested her most. Her answer was a desire to become fluent in German, English, and Arabic, with the aim of becoming either a translator or possibly a journalist.

Ben could see that Georges was beginning to look rather left out. Turning to him he asked if *he* wanted to learn any other languages, to which he replied that English was enough of a challenge at the moment and he could even do with improving his French! Ben asked how they had met, which caused them to laugh. Georges said it was by accident, literally. He had been casually walking to this café when he was hit by a young woman riding a motor scooter and knocked off his feet. He wasn't badly hurt, but nevertheless was happy to let the young lady fuss over him. Georges told Ben with a wink that he probably over-acted, but it was worth it. He managed somehow to get the young lady to park her scooter and have a coffee with him, and from there a romance grew.

The time seemed to fly by and Odette yawned, which signalled to Ben that it was time to go. After an argument with Georges over who was to pay the bill, finally deciding to pay half each, he said goodnight and headed back to the hotel. As he walked back, he thought what a good life he had; if only he could share it more with Sophie.

The year passed in a hectic but fairly lonely way for Ben as his phone links with England became routine. His homesickness had become manageable and he resigned himself to the fact that he wouldn't see those at home for some time. One big cloud that loomed ever nearer was the thought of spending Christmas away from family. Still, he thought that if he could get through that, the New Year might bring changes for the better.

A little humour was experienced by the kitchen staff at the expense of a commis chef. It was the young guy who Gabrielle had set her sights on. He had disappeared and nobody seemed to know where he had gone. He appeared at the kitchen door a week later with two of the most beautiful black eyes Ben had ever seen. His nose was not as straight as it used to be and the split on his lip meant that he wouldn't be doing any whistling for some time. Ben grinned at Georges and they shook hands; *that could have been me,* Ben thought, if Georges had not put him wise to Gabrielle's ploys.

Craig Hinson called a meeting of all the chefs at the end of November to let them know what was planned in the month ahead. He informed them that the hotel was almost fully booked for the season. It would be hosting a round of office parties, family-get-togethers, and the Marché de Noel, that in itself would mean a lot of extra work. Hinson told them that time off would be restricted. Chefs with families would be given priority in granting time off, particularly over the Christmas week. It was nothing new to the chefs, who were used to working when others were enjoying themselves – that was the life they had chosen. Hinson called Ben into his office when the meeting had finished.

'I'm sorry, Ben, that we can't let you go over the holidays. However, there is a place at our table at my home and you are more than welcome. In fact my daughters have insisted that you spend Christmas with us.'

It was an offer Ben had no desire to refuse. 'Thanks, Craig, that would be wonderful. Do you want me to give you a hand with the cooking?'

'Heaven forbid, my wife would kill me! She's in charge of the kitchen and woe betide anyone who tries to interfere with her preparation and cooking.'

Ben asked Georges what he would be doing at Christmas and his nervous reply was that he had been invited to spend time with Odette and her parents.

'I am très inquiet – that is very worried.'

'What's up, Georges?'

'I have met them only once and her papa he scares me. He is like schoolmaster and looks at me as if I am schoolboy.'

Ben laughed. 'I'm quite sure you'll be fine.'

'I hope so, I hope so.'

Before the season got underway, Georges asked Ben if he would like to meet at the café again with him and Odette. Ben jumped at the chance to be with friends, and chatting would take his mind off what he was missing at home. Odette had asked Georges if she should get a girl friend to join them, but Georges had seen the way Ben looked when he spoke of home and Sophie.

'I think it may be bad idea. I think maybe Ben get upset and put him in difficult position.' They agreed that just the two of them would go, and Odette said she would buy Ben a little something for Christmas.

They met in the same café and talked of the month ahead. Ben told them of his dilemma, which involved finding presents for Sophie and his aunt. He looked pleadingly at Odette and asked if she would help him choose the gifts for the women in his life. Odette was eager and ready; if there was one thing she enjoyed it was shopping, especially for others. She would let her imagination run wild, she declared, but would remember it was not her money she was spending!

After dragging both men around a host of shops it was decided that Ben should buy gold chains for his aunt and Sophie. Sophie's chain could be worn around the neck and the one for his aunt as a bracelet. Odette had been excellent in finding the best valued items and Ben knew he could not have done it without her. The shops were one thing, but Odette and Georges also dragged Ben around the Christmas market at Place d'Erlon. The market had only opened the day before and all the stalls were bursting with goods. The lights alone were fantastic. Ben had never seen anything like it and the crowd was a complete European melting pot. Ben heard all sorts spoken; French, German, Dutch, and importantly for him, some English speakers. After they had finished, they collapsed into the seats of a café and enjoyed a well-earned cup of strong coffee.

Advent calendars appeared in shop windows together with postcards from Père Noel. The first windows in the calendars were opened and Christmas began. Fortunately, it was too busy for Ben to dwell on what he might be missing. Presents had arrived from home and he had made sure that those he had bought Sophie and his aunt were in the post in time to reach them before Christmas. Ben had not appreciated what Christmas Eve meant to the French. Georges had explained to him that Le Réveillon meant 'time for awakening' and it was traditional to have a copious meal with all the family that lasted late into the evening. This normally happened on Christmas Eve, but lots of people now preferred the meal on Christmas Day.

Work in the kitchen was hard and very hot. Parties came and went, businesses gave their workers an evening out, the Christmas fair was a huge attraction and the hotel was full to bursting. Ben's phone calls to Sophie were not that long as he had been known to fall asleep during a conversation and she had to shout down the phone to keep his attention.

On Christmas day he headed to Craig Hinson's house. Craig's wife was busy in the kitchen with their daughters, preparing the meal. Craig was making sure the tree was in good order and the presents were neatly placed beneath it. It was not all his wife's doing. Craig had been hard at work the previous night getting everything ready so that his wife could concentrate on the main items. In good time, the Hinson household together with Ben sat down to a feast. The chatter was mainly in French, but the girls continued to practise their English on Ben. There was a good deal of laughter, and together with excellent food the evening sped by. Craig took Ben to one side and asked if he would like to use his phone to contact England. Ben jumped at the chance. There was a telephone in the sitting room and Ben was left alone to make his call. He knew the number off by heart and was pleased to get through straight away. His aunt and uncle were over the moon that he had found time to call on Christmas Day. Sadly, Sophie was with her father, but his aunt said she would be at their house on Boxing Day.

'Don't let her go anywhere until I have called,' he pleaded.

'I'll nail her feet to the floor!' his aunt jokingly replied.

Ben said his goodbyes to the Hinson family and made his way back to the hotel. He felt good, but as he walked sadness seemed to creep up on him as he thought of what they would be doing back home. He could see his aunt and uncle with friends having opened their presents and watched the Queen, collapsing into their chairs and falling into a satisfied sleep. He wondered what Sophie was doing at home with her father, hopefully enjoying herself as best she could. Would she be thinking of him? Of course she would.

As he passed windows with lights shining brightly, he also tried to visualise what Georges would be doing. Was he getting on alright with Odette's father or would he be saying very little, frightened by his presence? He would definitely have to quiz him the next time they met.

The following day, Boxing Day, Ben phoned his uncle's number. It was answered by a very excited Sophie. 'Oh Ben, I wish you could have been home for Christmas, I missed you so much.'

'Did you get the present ok?'

'Ben, you have been terrible, did it cost a lot, or shouldn't I ask.'

'You shouldn't ask, but do you like it?'

'I'm wearing it now and I don't want to ever take it off.'

Ben told Sophie about his time with the Hinson's and how he had missed her and the family, and promised he would make it up to her. Sophie became a little more serious when she said that she and Sarah had been talking and they were thinking of paying him a visit in the early spring.

His mouth dropped open. 'You mean you will come and see me in France?'

'Yes, it'll be alright, I'll be in your aunt's safe hands.'

'What do you want me to do?'

There was an intake of breath on the other end of the phone. 'We haven't got very far with our plans at the moment. All we know is that we want to come over in March or April.'

After a moment's thought Ben said, 'Think about Easter but try to avoid the Easter weekend.'

Sophie hadn't really thought about Easter but it was something she would discuss with Sarah. They carried on talking until they had both exhausted their news. Ben ended the call asking Sophie to let him know as soon as possible any dates that they decided upon.

After the Christmas celebrations, January and February were dull and grey. Rain clouds kept coming in and snow fell. The city of Rheims looked wonderful with a layer of fresh snow and a star-filled sky. The workload in the kitchen seemed to drop off and Ben thought that this was possibly the best time for Sophie and his aunt to visit, but it wasn't particularly good for Ben's aunt who had a great deal of work to do regarding the family business, and this was the time of year to get it into shape before the end of the financial year.

Ben's role in the kitchen changed as he became ever more proficient in the stations he worked on. Hinson had been impressed with Ben ever since he arrived and had followed his progress closely. It was decided that Ben should take on the role of 'chef de tournant'. This would put him under quite a lot of pressure, moving around different stations in the kitchen, filling absences due to sickness or holidays. It was also a good opportunity to serve in a management as well as a cook capacity, so he had to learn about dealing with people, which included building up his communication skills.

A bright spark of light came when Sophie told Ben that they had agreed on the dates they would visit. The next question was whether he could get the same time off. After discussing it with Hinson, it was agreed that Ben could take two long weekends to fit in with the dates Sophie had put forward. Unfortunately, the Durocort was at bursting point on the dates suggested, so they would have to find another place to stay. Ben thought this was not a bad outcome because if they stayed at the Durocort it would cost them an arm and a leg. He asked if Georges knew of any decent, inexpensive hotels and was grateful when one of the reception girls told him her sister worked at a small hotel called 'Belle Époque' on the Rue Chabaud.

Ben visited the hotel and was very impressed by the price they asked; it was a good deal. It was furnished in art deco style which he thought both Sophie and his aunt would enjoy. He reserved two single rooms, just in case Sophie wanted to be alone with him … or was that wishful thinking on his part?

The beginning of March saw a change in the weather. The rain eased and the skies brightened. Sophie and Sarah set off from London in a state of excitement and nerves. Sarah had to keep Sophie's feet on the ground, and also had to build her confidence when boarding the ferry. The Channel posed a problem. It was on the choppy side, a little rough, and Sophie became quite sick as they crossed. Fortunately, by the time they reached Calais, Sarah had managed to clean Sophie up and calm her down. Their train journey had its moments too, especially changing trains in Paris. Sarah had schoolgirl French, which didn't help much, but somehow, to their great relief, they managed to get the train for Rheims.

Ben met them at Rheims central station to the excitement and joy of all, and got them into a cab. They arrived at their hotel absolutely shattered, and Ben proposed to let them get settled in and call for them the following morning. He had planned the time they had available, and with the help of Georges and Odette he hoped he would be able to give both Sophie and Sarah an interesting time. It was Odette who proved to be a godsend; she organised visits to all the places of interest, the cathedral, the Palais du Tau, the Museum of Fine Arts, and of course lots of things to do with champagne. Ben's two long weekends meant that he could be with them most of the time while Odette literally took over and chaperoned them around the city.

They spent their evenings eating in various restaurants, and one evening they splashed out and ate at the Durocort. Sophie was eager to tell Ben all the news and gossip from home which included an update of the affair between Annabel and Peter Russell, which seemed to be developing into something serious.

As she spoke, she toyed with the gold chain she wore round her neck. Ben saw it and was delighted that she liked it so much.

Sophie noticed Ben looking at the chain. 'Recognise it?'

'Of course. It looks good on you, Sophie.'

She smiled. 'It would have been better if you'd been at home to give it to me yourself.'

'You're here now, Sophie, and that's all that matters.' He held her hand and gently ran his fingers along hers.

Sarah told Ben how Steven had decided to diversify and invest in the transportation of vegetables rather than retailing them. This came about because he could see how the supermarkets were encroaching on the small high street businesses and could foresee that his shops would soon be a thing of the past. He and a business friend had got together and invested in several refrigerated lorries. If all went well, they would build a fleet of vehicles and supply the main supermarkets.

While Odette and Sophie were shopping, Sarah took Ben to one side. 'Ben what do you think about your uncle and me offering Sophie a job?'

'What sort of job would it be? You know she's got this thing about being a hotel manager like Annabel Stewart.'

'That's what's stopping us asking her. We didn't want her to feel any obligation to work for the family firm.'

'I think Sophie knows her own mind well enough to make the right move. You never know, she might want a change in career, but to be perfectly honest, I don't think she does.'

'That's what I wanted to know.' Sarah was pleased. She didn't want to put any pressure on Sophie and decided to leave things as they were.

The visit proved to be a resounding success. Sophie and Sarah had been wined and dined, shown the delights of Rheims, and most of all they had all been together. Sophie and Ben could physically see and touch each other as opposed to being on the end of a telephone wire. Odette and Georges were fascinated by the joy Sophie and Sarah brought into Ben's life.

All too soon it was time for them to go. It had been good – too good, Ben thought as he saw them off at the station, and his mood darkened. How long would it be until he could get home? For chrissakes they were only just across the Channel – but it may as well have been Timbuctoo. And it was always a problem getting the time off. Back in his room he lay back and listened to his records and tried not to succumb to despair.

When Sophie reached home, she told her father all about the trip and that one day she would take him to Rheims. His response was that he was getting a little long in the tooth to be gallivanting across the Channel.

'You would really love it – the cathedral, the cafés, and the champagne.' Oh, the champagne, she could almost taste it again.

Her dad merely replied, 'One day, Sophie, perhaps one day.'

Sophie's working life at the hotel was progressing. She had been diligently studying for her exams and been successful. Her boss, Annabel, was very pleased and had taken Sophie on full time in the hotel reception. She was very pleased to get away from waitressing; no more customer complaints or the occasional dirty old man trying to grab her. She had, meanwhile, become fascinated by the relationship between Annabel and Detective Inspector Peter Russell, and observed them as he was led on by Annabel. She had a gift with men and was able to twist them round her little finger. Sophie was aware, though, that this seemed to be more than her usual casual fling. Something more serious was developing between them but she had been unable to discover exactly how serious.

19

Peter Russell and his team had been tackling quite a few drug-related cases as their remit had widened. Drug trafficking had become a serious problem, and not only locally or nationally but internationally. Peter had been dealing with Interpol and the US authorities, but even with the cooperation of many police forces he could not track down the main sources of the drug trade. It seemed as if they could up-sticks and move at the drop of a hat, leaving behind them a trail of horror. He and his team had become hardened to the facts surrounding drug abuse. They had witnessed the worst of outcomes, the death by overdose, the accidental taking of the wrong drug at the wrong time, and kids who just did not know what they were getting into. There still remained one case on his desk that rankled; his first case, the death of Max Steyning.

They had managed to trace his activities to off-shore bank accounts and a network of minor dealers, but he knew that there must be something he had missed that would give him the satisfaction of putting the case in the 'case closed' drawer. In the meantime, he had plenty to get on with and his private life had become a little more active since meeting Ms Stewart. He had taken her out a few times and they had had several meals in the hotel, which always brought a smile to the face of the young lady behind reception. It was Sophie who had taken his last reservation for dinner with Annabel, and he could see she was clearly curious, but thought better of asking questions. Instead, she observed Peter unobtrusively as he met Annabel and politely kissed the cheek she offered him.

The summer sun became a little stronger as the year moved on and Ben's life in Rheims became comfortable, which in some ways was not what he wanted. He wanted to maintain his yearning to go home and establish himself as a chef in London. He had made good friends with Georges and Odette and they kept him sane. It must have been two months after Sophie's visit that Ben was called into Hinson's office.

'Is there a problem?' Ben looked worried. It was unusual to be called into Hinson's office without some sort of fore-warning.

Craig signalled to Ben to sit. 'We have a bit of a dilemma, Ben' Hinson began. 'The chef that you exchanged with has had some personal problems – his grandmother has passed away and his mother is not in the best of health. His father is trying to keep things going but says he needs his son to help him deal with his mother's condition.' Ben was really worried now – he had no idea what this would mean for him. Hinson continued, 'You've been with me ... for how long?'

Ben calculated for a few seconds. 'It must be getting on for two years.'

'Yes, and I think you've done an excellent job. In fact, you have now reached a stage where I think you're ready to take up a position as chef de partie or even sous chef in a large hotel in London such as the Rosegarth.' They both sat in silence for a moment. 'I'll be very sorry to lose you, Ben, but maybe it is time for your placement here to come to an end. What do you think?'

'It's a bit sudden, and quite honestly I had no thought of going back permanently for at least another six months, but if it's a question of family, I know that if the boot was on the other foot, I would expect everyone concerned to help, so I will fit in with whatever is best.'

'Ben, it will be quite a quick move. The chef who swapped with you, Claud, wants to get back to his parents by the end of next month and that's only six weeks away. We can manage that here at the Durocort if it's ok with you.'

Ben's mind was in overdrive; he would have to get himself together and think of what needed to be done. It would be easier going home than coming to work in France, of course. He supposed it would be just a matter of packing his bags and saying goodbye. A panicky thought flashed across his mind. 'I hope you're saying that there will be a job for me at the Rosegarth.'

'Absolutely. There is no question about that, Ben.'

Ben felt a huge sense of relief.

Hinson continued, 'I have had a long chat with David Burdett and he said he would welcome you back with open arms and that he will sort out a suitable position for you.' He went through what had to be done to make Ben's return home as smooth as possible, and he asked Ben to stay until Claud arrived back. Again, he had cleared this with David Burdett. Ben could see little problem in that, and his main concern now was to let his family and Sophie know what was going on. Hinson told Ben to think about what had been said and to come back to him with any problems. Ben asked if a date had been set for Claud's return.

'Everyone concerned would like Claud to return here on the last day of July, and for you to return to England at the end of the second week of August. How does that sound?'

Ben's head was still spinning, but he managed, 'That sounds fine.' It would take him a few hours to adjust to what had just been discussed.

Hinson held out his hand and as he shook Ben's he said, 'Good, that's great, and I think that my wife and girls will want a visit from you before you go, so make sure you build that into your plans!'

Smiling, Ben left Hinson's office and walked back to his station shaking his head. He knew it would be a few hours before things sank in and then the fun would start. He looked round the kitchen and spotted Georges. What was he going to tell him and his lovely girlfriend, Odette? They had been good friends and he would miss them badly. The kitchen had become not only his place of work but somewhere things happened. It had been where he had learnt so much and seen so many things take place, it would be like leaving a second family.

He caught up with Georges at the end of service. They walked along the street in front of the hotel and Ben began to tell Georges what he had discussed with Hinson and how he was going to miss everyone and everything about the hotel.

'You not want stay in France?' Georges asked.

'If I had my way, I would spend time in both England and France, but some things are just not possible.'

Georges could see that Ben had split loyalties, but could understood that family, and especially Sophie, came first.

'You know we shall all miss you, even Gabrielle,' he said. They both had a good laugh as they remembered the problems Ben had had with her and the state of the commis chef after Gabrielle's husband had finished with him.

Ben looked up at the front of the hotel. 'This has been my home and I shall never forget it.' He told Georges he had about six weeks before he finished and that he intended to make every minute count.

Georges could see he meant what he said. 'We must meet

for drink – evening out – you, me, and Odette before you go.'

They went their separate ways, Ben to his room and Georges to see Odette and tell her of Ben's plans to leave. He knew she would be upset; she had enjoyed Ben's company and Sophie's too when she visited. But life goes on, changes happen, he thought philosophically.

Ben got to his room, sat down with paper and pen and did what his aunt would do – he made a list. It didn't turn out to be a long list. The main points were to let everyone know what was happening, to get his return journey sorted out, and to make sure there were no loose ends. He looked at his calendar. Six weeks had sounded a reasonable length of time, but when he thought about it now, it didn't seem that long at all.

The following morning Craig Hinson gathered everyone together in the kitchen. 'I have news for you all. I am sorry to say that we shall be losing an asset – but gaining another at the same time.' He stopped and looked around the faces of his brigade. 'The exchange we made with our sister hotel in London will be coming to an end shortly. Ben will be returning to England, and Claud, who of course you all know, will be bringing the new-found knowledge that he has gained in London, to us.'

There was a murmur from the chefs. The majority had worked with Claud and knew him as an energetic and committed commis chef as well as being a likeable guy. Hinson thought that it was going to be interesting to see how Claud fitted back in after his training at the Rosegarth. Similarly, he hoped that Ben would take something a little special from the experience he had gained in Hinson's kitchen.

'When will this happen?' a voice from the group asked.

'Claud will be returning to us on the last day of July and Ben will be leaving in mid August, so plenty of time for you to buy him a farewell gift.' This caused some laughter. Hinson was pleased with the reaction of the staff in the kitchen. Ben had been popular mainly because of his skill and work rate. However, he had really only made one true friend and that was Georges.

On the top of Ben's list was a note to phone his aunt and uncle, so as soon as he could get to the phone he dialled his uncle's number. His aunt answered.

'Hello?' It was her telephone voice, not too posh but more formal than her normal relaxed tones.

Ben didn't waste any time coming to the point. 'Aunty, it's me and I'll be coming home in the middle of August!'

'What! For how long for?' she asked.

'For good.'

'WHAT? Her voice was now full of questions.

'There has been a development which means my exchange will be finishing in August.' Ben realised he would have to spell out all the whys and wherefores so he took a deep breath and told her everything. At the end of his explanation he paused, giving his aunt time to let the news sink in.

'Tell me the dates again.' He could imagine her reaching for her diary.

'Oh, Ben, this is such good news. Do you want me to tell Sophie or would you like me to get her here so you can tell her yourself tomorrow?'

'If you could arrange for her to be with you tomorrow at this time, I'll call again. I really would like to tell her myself if you can you keep a secret like this from her!'

'I'll have you know I can keep secrets with the best of them,' she exclaimed indignantly.

'Ok, great. I've got to go now but I'll speak to you again tomorrow.' With that he hung up. He felt quite exhausted. He didn't know why that was, but every time he talked to his aunt about anything important it took it out of him.

There was nothing he could really do that night so he went out to a local café and ordered 'un verre de bierre' and something to eat; he wanted to be on his own so that he could digest this new turn of events. The day had been one of surprise and excitement and Ben thought he was ready to get things moving.

In the kitchen the mood seemed to be a little lighter than usual – Ben hoped it wasn't because he was on the move!

Georges grabbed his arm and pulled him to one side. 'Can you come to Odette's house for meal on Friday night?'

'To Odette's house? Why not the cafe?'

'It's Odette's mother and father – she has told them about you and they want to meet you before you return to the UK.'

'Yes, ok, should be alright, I think.'

'Good,' said Georges, 'I will let them know.'

That was another thing for Ben to put in his diary. The calendar on his wall was getting quite full. Craig Hinton had suggested several dates to Ben for a meal at his house and they had agreed on a Sunday which suited them both.

'This time I will cook the meal.' Hinton smiled at Ben. 'You can keep my wife and daughters amused.'

Days flew by and the meal with Odette's family loomed. Ben didn't know what to expect, although Georges had told him about the Christmas he had spent with Odette's parents and they seemed easy enough to get on with. The day arrived and Ben dutifully dressed in his best shirt and trousers. He considered wearing a tie but decided against it; he wanted to feel relaxed, not choked.

The evening was a success even though the conversation was a little stilted. It varied in complexity from part French and part English to French with a smattering of Egyptian, but they all seemed to understand each other with the use of sign language and a certain amount of guess work. Ben made his farewells and promised to keep in touch with Odette and her parents, who were very keen to keep abreast of what was going on in the UK. Ben thought, *one down and one to go.*

By the time the meal with the Hinson's came round, Ben was becoming anxious about his journey home. Six weeks had become three and Claud was due back the following week. He felt at home with the Hinson's, whose house was full of family things, and the way they treated him was like one of the family. The girls kept him on his toes. They wanted him not only to play games but also to tell them all about England. All three had an infectious laugh, which to Ben sounded like a loud giggle.

It was a long day. They didn't sit down to dinner until 7:30 pm, which could be considered early by some. Craig Hinson had surpassed himself. Starting with a glass of champagne, Ben knew he was in for a treat and he wasn't disappointed. Hors d'oeuvres of fig and goats-cheese tartlets were followed by sweet duck breasts in a cherry sauce with a pea and carrot salad. It was the fine points that Hinson had perfected, a fine drizzle of honey or some toasted pumpkin seed oil. The cheese board was fantastic. Ben had become a great fan of French cheese and Hinson served up a selection of nine different ones. The wines that accompanied each course had been selected with care, and were perfect.

It was the final course that, despite being almost too full to eat it, Ben thought was the most fascinating – a simple Tarte au Citron. It looked so uncomplicated, but to produce something as perfect as that took a chef with a great deal of skill. It was gorgeous – light, bursting with flavour, and such a complement to the richness of the meal. For the girls he had made separate glasses of sweet Café Liegeois. They looked amazing and the girls squealed with pleasure as Hinson brought them to the table.

What a success, Ben thought, as he said farewell to the girls and Hinson's wife. They had provided Ben with a sense of home for which he would be ever grateful; he would not forget them.

20

As the month drew to an end, Ben felt an enormous sense of regret at leaving the Durocort, but the planning of his journey home filled him with excited anticipation. Claud arrived back at the hotel and was met with a warm welcome. Hinson made time and had Ben and Claud together in his office. They talked about how things differed between the two hotels, the style of cooking and the general running of an English kitchen compared to a French one. Claud admitted he was glad to be back and looking forward to re-joining his team in the kitchen. Georges had previously worked with Claud and respected him as a chef, but they hadn't developed the friendship that he had with Ben. However, Georges was able and willing to work with Claud and they both got on well enough with each other in the kitchen.

Later, as Ben was standing lost in thought, Georges came up noiselessly and stood beside him, which startled him.

George laughed. 'It's a joke my brother and I played on each other when we were children, and sometimes when we are together, we still play!'

'You scared me, I didn't hear you at all.' Georges wanted to check with Ben about a trip to the café to meet with him and Odette.

'This weekend would be good for me,' Ben told him.

'Is good, yes, but maybe Friday better because of my shift,' he replied, and they agreed a time for their meeting.

It was the penultimate weekend and Ben knew it would be hard saying goodbye to Georges and Odette. The evening was full of laughter as they talked about the times they had spent in each other's company. Georges asked Ben if there was anything he regretted about leaving.

'There is one thing. I've seen a lot of Rheims, but I've only ever seen Paris as a traveller passing through, and I always promised myself I would see the sights of Paris before I went back to England.'

The following day Georges knocked on Craig Hinson's office door. Georges felt at ease with his head chef and without hesitation asked him if he could possibly have the next Thursday, Friday, and Saturday off.

Hinson was curious. 'May I ask why?' He had a peculiar way of raising an eyebrow when asking questions, which tended to make people think twice before putting their question.

'Ben has never properly seen Paris and I would like to take him there and show him some of the sights.' Georges waited for a response. Hinson smiled and looked up at his year planner.

'I think we can cope without you for a couple of days. As long as you don't lead him astray it should be manageable!'

Georges had a brief chat with one of the receptionists; she was able to recommended a cheap hotel which he should have no problem in booking for three nights.

'Ah, Ben.' Georges approached his friend with an excited look on his face and an air of mystery. 'How would you like have guided tour of Paris before you go back to England?' Georges' English had improved very much over the past year but he still had difficulty with certain words, and those he did know well sounded strange with his heavy accent.

'Wow, I would like that very much,' Ben replied. 'But how and when?'

'The week before you return to England. I will arrange all. If you are ok, we shall have good time.'

Ben laughed as he clapped his friend on the back, and they made their way to the kitchen. Georges had a busy evening. After he had finished his shift, he got on the phone first to the hotel recommended by the receptionist, the hotel Belle Époque,' and booked a twin room for three nights. Money was tight and they were good friends so he was sure that sharing would not be a problem. Once the hotel was booked, his next call was to his brother. Theo answered the phone in his soft low voice which always made Georges feel good. He explained his plans and Theo said that they would have to make a night of it; he would arrange a get-together with some of his friends and they would make sure his English friend would remember Paris for the rest of his life. Times and places were agreed, and Georges was satisfied that he had got a good plan together.

The dishes Ben prepared became fewer as Claud took over from him. He was getting to become a spare part, not really needed, so he would float around helping wherever he could. Georges recognised the fact that his friend was lost without a proper job and kept his spirits up by telling him where they would go when they reached the greatest city on earth. Ben didn't dispute what he said, but in his heart he knew that, for him, London would rank above Paris.

On the Wednesday before their trip, Ben said his goodbyes to those who he wouldn't see again before leaving. It was a more emotional experience than he had anticipated. There were some good characters in the kitchen, only one or two who got on his nerves, and he hoped they held him in the same light.

Thursday arrived and Ben had got his belongings together. He made sure that all his precious items were packed safely, leaving out only what he wanted for his trip to Paris and his journey home. He would change when he returned from Paris and would have to take some dirty clothes home, but he was sure that his aunt wouldn't hold it against him.

Georges came to the hotel to meet Ben and together they made their way to the station.

'What shall we do until we reach Paris?' Ben asked Georges.

'You teach me more English. I need good English for when I come see you in London!' They both smiled at the thought of Georges in London.

'You are welcome at any time, and I will show you the sights of London and we can see which is the better city.'

They talked about their lives, and most importantly their loves. The more Ben spoke of Sophie the more he wanted to see her. *It won't be long*, he told himself.

They reach the Gare du Nord as it was getting dark. Georges said they would get a taxi to the hotel, a special treat. The hotel was set alongside the Canal St Martin, not the finest of areas but good enough for them. After going through the necessary booking-in and registering, they went to their room and quickly unpacked their bits and pieces. Georges said he would find them a low-price place to eat. They managed to find a small Italian restaurant within walking distance of the hotel and took their time over plates of pasta.

'Not as good as ours,' Ben grinned. The conversation had to be about food and how it was prepared.

'What would you like to do tomorrow?' Georges asked.

Ben was gazing out of the restaurant window, watching people walking by at a leisurely pace.

Georges' voice brought him back to reality. 'Sorry, Georges, what did you say?'

Georges grinned and repeated his question.

'Perhaps Les Champs Elysees and the Arc de Triomphe?'

Georges nodded. 'Then we must go to 'Hotel des Invalides' and see the tomb of Napoleon. He may not be one of your country's heroes but he still is one of ours.'

'That sounds good.' Ben sipped the chianti that he had bought by the glass. 'Um, not very good, but it will do. What I would also like to see is some of the really grand hotels. I know that sounds crazy, but I have heard so much about hotels like George Cinq and the Hôtel le Bristol, I would just like to walk along the Rue de Rivoli and soak up the atmosphere of the city.'

Georges smiled. 'Ben, we 'ave only two days! What you want to see take us much much longer.'

Ben was in a dream world of his own. 'What about the Mona Lisa? I have just got to see her.'

'We can try, Ben, but the queues are very long and because we have little time maybe we leave her for another day.'

On the following day, Georges initiated Ben to the delights of the Paris Metro. Ben was expecting a similar sort of system as the London Underground and he wanted to see if people spoke to each other or whether they just sat and read newspapers like they did on the tubes. The chatter was mainly from tourists, so very much the same as London.

The day went well. They ate in the Champs Elysees just for the sheer hell of it. Georges then insisted they had coffee in a café halfway along the Avenue Victor Hugo where they could 'people watch'. He took Ben to the George Cinq, which impressed him a lot, and then to the Rue de Rivoli where Ben passed more grand hotels.

As he and Georges were walking past the frontage of the Hotel Renaissance, Ben thought he saw a figure he recognised. *It couldn't be.* But it looked for all the world like the bodyguard who had served the meals at Steyning's house. Ben had to shake his head, and as he glanced back, he was sure that the man looked directly at him. He shivered, took Georges' arm and led him quickly across the street.

'What's wrong?' Georges asked.

'I think I've seen somebody who scares me.'

Ben glanced back and could not see the man, but he felt sure he had been seen and recognised.

The man Ben referred to as the bodyguard had indeed recognised him and knew that Ben had seen him. He followed Ben and his companion at a discrete distance until they went into a café. He spotted a phone booth and made his way unobtrusively towards it. His call was brief. He told the voice on the other end that a loose end had turned up which needed dealing with.

'Can you handle it or do you need help?' He told the voice that he did not need help and it would be resolved within twenty-four hours. The bodyguard had plenty of time. He would wait until an opportunity presented itself and then do whatever was necessary to protect him and other members of his group.

It had been a good day and Ben had fulfilled an ambition. Georges told him there was more to come and that the next day they would pay a visit to the Sacré Coeur. He would also show him the Moulin Rouge in Montmartre, although it would not be open at that time, and Ben could pick up some small souvenirs in the markets to take home. Georges said they would take the Metro to the Place de la Concorde and walk along the river Seine. Ben was delighted and grateful that Georges was able to show him so much. He was, however, still uneasy about having glimpsed the American from Steyning's house and kept looking around him. When they returned to their hotel he still felt anxious, although he was sure he had not been followed and that he had nothing to worry about. He told Georges of his fears and he said to forget it – nothing was going to spoil their time in Paris.

At the end of their second day of playing tourist, Georges told Ben that they were expected at his brother's apartment and that it had been arranged for a gathering of his brother's friends to have a small party. Ben saw the look on Georges' face when he said 'small' and wondered what he meant by small.

It was getting on for seven that evening when Georges said that they had better get ready to go. The weather was warm so there was no need for coats. Both wore flared Levi jeans and rather similar shirts with t-shirts under them. The fashion was more for brightly patterned, long-collared shirts which they both thought were not for them, so they took to wearing plain or basic check shirts with the new trend of button-down collars.

They left the hotel feeling good and looking forward to a very interesting evening. It was the Metro again. Ben felt he had seen enough of underground trains for the day but followed dutifully behind Georges as he bought a 'carnet' of tickets. The stops they passed were new to Ben and he tried to keep up with the names by following the Metro map on the carriage wall.

Georges gave Ben a nudge. 'Where we are going is not high class.' Ben looked at him quizzically. 'Is not pretty and some bad people living there.'

Georges' English may have left a lot to be desired but Ben understood what he was trying to tell him.

'My brother, he lives in part of Paris tourists do not visit unless they want see the Basilica of Saint-Denis.'

'What is the Basilica?' Ben asked.

'It is a place where the old kings and queens of France are buried.'

'We have Saint George's Chapel in Windsor Castle, perhaps it's similar.'

'Very good name for such a place.' Georges smiled. 'Please, Ben, you must not think everyone bad who lives in this sort of place. There some good places too and some very good people who live there.'

'My mind is open and I will see what I see!'

Ben hadn't realised just how far it was to Saint Denis. It took them the best part of an hour to get to the end of the line. The station was well lit, the white walls reflecting the neon lights, which made Ben's eyes hurt. Georges led the way to the street. It was an area that was undergoing change; everywhere there were construction sites, new buildings completed and occupied, plus older structures that were probably in line for demolition. Some of the buildings had been erected with narrow passageways, which did not look inviting.

They arrived at Theo's apartment and Georges made the introductions. 'Ben, this is Theo. Theo, this is Ben,' and repeated it in French.

Ben held out his hand, uttering his well-practised greeting: 'Heureux de faire votre connaissance.' This pleased Theo, who then burst into French leaving Ben in a daze. He could tell that the word he would use most that evening would be 'lentement'!

Fortunately Georges was by his side to interpret when he couldn't keep up. 'My brother is very glad meet you and has good evening prepared for you.'

'Merci.'

Theo turned to Georges and started to tell him what was planned. Ben could follow most of what was said and gathered that they would go to a café where they would meet some good friends. Georges informed Ben that Theo's friends were some people he had helped get to France from Algeria after the French had left the country.

The sun was still up as they left Theo's apartment block, but the tall buildings cast long shadows which made the streets feel more menacing. They had walked for about fifteen minutes when they came to an older, rather run-down building which boasted a cafe on its ground floor. The sign above the doors and windows showed in large bold lettering 'Café des Amis' which stood out on a maroon background. There were two large glass windows either side of a glazed door. The window to the right proudly announced 'RESTAURANT' and below it À LA CARTE. The door bore the proprietor's name, and on the window to the left, in someone's rather clumsy handwriting, 'crêpes à tous les heures', and in bold capitals 'VINS DE PROPRIETAIRES'. The overall impression was of a long-established place where friends might gather for drinks and perhaps something to eat.

As Theo opened the door, a bell rang and those in the café turned their heads to see who the newcomers were. There were several loud good-natured greetings as Theo walked towards some of the men standing at the bar. Ben could see that these were the friends Theo had mentioned. In the centre of the café, tables had been arranged in one line and there was seating for about ten. Ben could see that the men were not drinking alcohol; soft drinks were the order of the day, so when asked what he would like he asked for a coke.

He was introduced to everyone and noticed that although the men spoke in French, they also lapsed into what sounded like Arabic. Theo took time to make sure Ben heard every one's name, although whether he would remember them was another matter. The group consisted entirely of men, and Ben wondered where the women were, but didn't like to ask.

Theo called for everyone to go to the table. Ben eyed the men as they took their seats. There seemed to be something unusual about them, but he couldn't put his finger on it until the man next to Georges looked directly at him. His eyes were blue, and after closer inspection Ben noticed his hair was not so much black as a lighter colour, a sort of mid-brown. Georges sat next to Ben and Theo pulled out a chair and plonked himself down on his other side. He could see that Ben had questions to ask.

'How come they have blue eyes and light brown hair?'

Theo could just about understand the question and with George's help, told Ben that they were from the Maghreb, the western part of North Africa, a region that included Morocco and Algeria amongst others. He explained that there were many who had different colouring from the rest of the countries of North Africa, although why this was the case was probably lost in history.

Ben said the obvious. 'You know them very well.'

'I met them some years ago when Georges and I lived in Marseilles. I had made many journeys to the coast of Africa to do business. Some of these people came to me to ask if I could help them get to France. They were in trouble with the Algerians after the country had separated from France.' He paused, then continued, 'These people were some of those who had worked for the French and had held not senior posts in the French administration but had nevertheless a certain amount of authority. When Algeria gained independence, those in any sort of powerful position fled to France, provided they had the money and contacts. Some, like my friends, found themselves alone and victimised by the new Algerian regime.'

During the conversation, Ben caught the word 'Harkis' and through Georges asked what it meant. He was told it was a name given to those who had fought alongside the French against the Algerian insurgents. Ben said he thought Theo had indicated they had administrative roles, and as he said this he looked again at the men around the table and thought to himself that they were the toughest looking clerks he had ever seen.

Theo continued. 'Once the new regime had been established, they had been rounded up. Their possessions were confiscated and their documents taken. My friends gathered together what they could to try and buy their way to France. I could do little for them myself, but I suggested some people who might be able to get them to France. What happened was that these persons took their money and left them high and dry without any means of getting to France.'

Theo paused to drink and talk to some of those close by. He told them he was giving Ben details of how they got to France. They looked at Ben and nodded their appreciation. Their escape from Algeria seemed to have been plagued with setbacks as the time of escape kept changing and the boat they were supposed to use didn't materialise. Details of how Theo eventually managed to get the eight people fleeing from Algeria to Paris were vague. All he would say was that he used business friends to help him. The initial eight arrived in Paris and started their exile in Saint Denis where they were forced to live in pretty poor conditions without any work or income. Through sheer determination they managed to survive. They started by delivering messages by bicycle and then went on to using motor scooters; eventually they were able to buy one car until they could accumulate funds, and now they had four vehicles and a steady stream of clients, although they were not strictly legal customers.

One of the men sitting close to Theo mentioned something and Theo looked up. 'My friends have also been able to get members of their families to Paris as well.'

Georges had done a marvellous job of translating this sordid story. Ben was intrigued by all that had been said. He now looked at Theo with admiration. What a guy!

21

The evening passed quickly. The food had been delicious and Ben would remember the flavour and aroma of the spices for a long time. All those around the table had been in good spirits all evening. Ben looked at his watch and then at Georges.

'We mustn't miss our last train.'

Georges repeated this to his brother who immediately turned to one of his friends. After a brief discussion, Theo told them that his good friend Hakim would drive them back to their hotel. Ben thanked Theo and Hakim but said it was late and that their hotel was quite a distance from Saint Denis. Theo spoke rapidly to Georges, who translated for Ben, the gist of it being that it was no problem as Hakim could do some business over there – it seemed there was always business to be done in Paris no matter what time of the day or night.'

Both Ben and Georges relaxed and continued their conversations with Theo and his friends. The party reached its natural conclusion and Theo's guests started to ready themselves to leave. After saying their farewells, Ben, Georges, Theo, and Hakim made their way to the door. As they reached the pavement in front of the café, Georges, Theo, and Hakim told Ben that they had forgotten to arrange something for the following month. Ben carried on and wandered slowly along the dimly lit street. He was content; he had had a good evening with good food and good company. He had walked about a hundred metres when Theo, Georges, and Hakim opened the café door. Theo could see Ben strolling unhurriedly ahead of him. He turned to Georges and Hakim and holding his finger to his lips indicated silence. Georges and Hakim stopped and watched as Theo started moving stealthily towards Ben. Georges smiled at Hakim – they both knew that Theo was going to give Ben the fright of his life by using all his skill to reach him without his noticing. Theo was lost from their view as he made his way as close to the wall of the buildings as he could, making sure he could not be heard.

Ben was thinking about his journey home, totally oblivious to what Theo was doing. As he walked along, he noticed a narrow passageway on his left – nothing remarkable in that, he just wondered where it led.

The bodyguard had been patient. He had followed Ben and Georges since first sighting them. It had been fairly simple until they reached Saint Denis, but even then he had managed to keep out of sight without anyone noticing him and had noted the café where they had spent the evening. He had waited in the passageway biding his time and working out what he would do if the opportunity arose. He had watched the door of the café and seen people leaving, and he suddenly spotted that the lad he had been following was walking towards him alone. This was his chance. The silk tie he was wearing was undone and he slipped it from his neck, winding an end around each hand. He flexed it and was happy with its strength; it would do. He stepped back into the passageway making sure he could not be seen by his target. It was two in the morning, there was nobody in sight and the street was empty. As Ben came closer, he readied himself and as Ben reached the edge of the passageway the bodyguard stepped out, wrapped the tie round Ben's neck and pulled.

Theo had by this time got to within two metres of Ben and was about to pounce when he saw the figure that suddenly stepped out of the shadows, put something around Ben's neck and start to pull his head backwards. Theo's hand went to his pocket and in one smooth action his knife was in his hand. The razor-sharp blade sprang from the handle and glinted in the dim light. Theo leaped forward, reached up slightly and drew the blade swiftly across the throat of Ben's attacker.

The blade moved easily as it severed the carotid artery. The assassin's arms began to try to disengage from the tie he had put round Ben's neck but it was wrapped round his hands and he couldn't free them. As the blood pumped from his neck, the man still tried to get his hands free in a frantic effort to stop the bleeding from his neck, but within seconds his arms started to weaken and his vision blurred. He fell back, taking Ben with him, and they both hit the ground, Ben ending up on top of the dying man. The fountain of blood from the man's neck started to ease as his eyes dimmed and his life sped away. Ben tried to roll away but he was still held against the body of the man by the tie wound around his neck.

Theo saw the problem, made his way carefully around the body and managed to prise the dead man's fingers open and release Ben from his grip. Ben managed to shift his body and crawl slightly to one side of the lifeless body. He was choking and holding his neck. The tie had not bitten deep into his flesh but it had hurt and his throat was painful. He tried to speak but nothing came out.

Theo barked out some commands and Georges and Hakim rushed forward. They each took one of Ben's arms and hauled him to his feet. It was not an easy task as Ben kept on falling, but eventually they managed to get him to stand upright. Theo could see that Ben was alright, and with a great sense of urgency he waved them all away.

'Allez, allez!'

They left Theo with the body, and as they moved hurriedly away from the scene Ben saw the face of his attacker and knew it was the person they had called the bodyguard. He was shaken by the sight of the contorted body, the dead blank eyes and twisted mouth. Half dragging Ben between them, they came to a turning and Hakim pulled Ben and Georges around the corner to a car parked outside a row of shops.

Before getting into the car, Hakim told Georges to take Ben's shirt off. It was covered in blood down one side and there was a certain amount on Ben's face and in his hair. As Georges fumbled with the buttons, Hakim pushed him roughly to one side, grabbed the two sides of the shirt and ripped it apart, buttons flying in all directions. Hakim pulled off the shirt and rolled it into a small ball, carefully avoiding any of the blood. Without ceremony he opened the back door and literally threw Ben onto the back seat. A rapid conversation passed between Hakim and Georges, the car started and Hakim pulled away.

Ben lay on the back seat struggling to regain his senses. What had happened in the last twenty minutes was a nightmare. His throat hurt, his eyes stung and he couldn't understand the conversation that was going on between Georges and Hakim. The last thing Ben could really remember was the face of the dead man, Theo whistling to the café, and men running towards him.

The lights of late-night Paris flashed by and Ben still lay on the back seat of the car. Hakim drew up in front of their hotel and as he opened the back door Ben struggled to sit upright. Georges reached in and helped him get to his feet. There was another burst of rapid French as Hakim started to get back behind the wheel.

'D'accord,' Georges responded. He took Ben's arm and helped him walk to the door of the hotel. Hakim's car disappeared into the night as Georges pushed open the entrance. As they walked in, the night porter looked up. He had seen many young men who had been out on the town returning after they had had too much to drink, and the dishevelled pair he saw were no different.

The lift rattled and shook a little as it made its way up to the third floor. Georges led the way, still keeping hold of Ben's arm. Georges could see that it would take Ben quite some time to get over what had happened that night. Ben collapsed onto his bed, physically and mentally exhausted. His lips were parched, and as he ran his tongue along them he noticed a taste that made him jump up and run for the bathroom – blood, not his blood but that of the dead man. Before he could help himself, he threw up all he had eaten and drunk that evening. Bent over the toilet, the vomit came through his mouth and his nose, his eyes almost popping out of his head; he couldn't stop, it just kept coming.

Eventually he gained control over his body and flushed the toilet several times. Looking in the mirror he could see specks of dried blood on his face and neck. In two frenzied minutes he had taken off the rest of his clothes and got into the shower. It took him a good ten minutes to convince himself that he had removed all traces of blood from his body. Grabbing his toothbrush, he scrubbed his teeth hard enough to make them bleed. The sight of his own blood made things still worse, and even after he had rinsed his mouth he could still taste blood, although at least it was his own. He gargled until the water from his mouth ran clear, and eventually he began to feel calmer. After drying himself he inspected himself again and was satisfied that none of the blood that had landed on him during the struggle was on his body, face, or neck. Grabbing a clean t-shirt, he lay down on his bed and tried to sleep. Georges asked him anxiously if he was alright; Ben could only grunt. They both tried to get some sleep but by six in the morning it had become a pointless exercise. It seemed as if the sun was mocking them as it rose higher in the sky.

'Breakfast?' Georges asked.

'I don't think I could eat anything.'

'Perhaps coffee?'

'Yes, coffee would be good.'

They made their way to a nearby café and Georges ordered. Ben's voice was still very hoarse and Georges could see it hurt when he tried to speak. After sipping some coffee, Ben asked Georges what time their train was due to depart for Rheims.

'We have three hours, we take our time, yes?' Ben nodded and looked up at the morning sun. He would be glad to get away from Paris and the quicker the better.

When they returned to their room Georges said he had to phone his brother, and settled himself down on the bed. Ben tried to follow the conversation but found in difficult to concentrate.

'Ben, my brother asks who was that man and why he want harm you?'

Speaking with difficulty, he told Georges slowly that he didn't know the man's name and all he knew was that he was linked to some serious drug dealers back in the UK. Georges' face had a look of total surprise on it as he passed the information to his brother.

'My brother asks what drugs?'

Ben tried to speak but could only cough. He drank some water and spluttered that he thought it was very hard drugs, like heroin and cocaine.

'My brother says this very bad but his friends will deal with the situation. But Ben, you not speak of last night to anyone. Est-ce que vous comprenez?'

'Oui, je comprends.'

Georges continued the conversation for several more minutes then hung up. 'My brother wants me make sure you know that if you speak of this it will mean terrible trouble for everyone.'

Ben closed his eyes. 'D'accord.'

The time came for them to go. Making sure they had everything with them, they went down to reception and Georges paid the bill. Ben would give him half later. Making their way on the Metro to their station, Ben felt vulnerable, as if he was being watched by everyone he passed. He kept pulling his shirt collar tight so that the bruising on his neck was not visible. Georges tried to make conversation but Ben seemed to be in a world of his own, and that world was not pleasant. Ben felt numb from the neck upwards. He couldn't focus on anything; his mind was devoid of ideas.

They negotiated their way to the Gard du Nord and boarded the train for Rheims. As they sat down, Georges looked at Ben, who avoided eye contact. When Georges spoke, he received no reply and so it went on until they reached Rheims Central station. Standing on the platform Georges made Ben drop his case and gripped his arms. 'Ben, you must speak. You will be going home tomorrow. You must try to forget what happened.'

Ben just picked up his case and started to walk towards the exit. Georges caught up with him and began to talk very urgently. 'Ben, is time for you to be you again. You must talk to me.'

Ben looked at Georges and shook his head. 'I can't, my head is still full of what happened.'

'That was yesterday,' insisted Georges fiercely. 'Today you have your world to face. Please try hard.'

'I will try, I promise you I will try.'

Georges managed to get a few more words out of Ben as they walked, but not much. It was awkward and stilted as they approached the Durocort.

Ben turned to Georges. 'I'm sorry, Georges, you've been wonderful. Just give me tonight and I promise I will be better in the morning.'

Georges was not convinced and he knew that Ben needed to have his head fully sorted out if he was to make it back to England the day after tomorrow. He made sure that Ben reached his room and watched him start to unpack his case.

'I will come see you tomorrow. Please try get some sleep. À'demain.'

Georges left Ben still with his mind not quite functioning. Ben looked around his room, rested his head on his chest and cried. He didn't know why he cried but it felt good to let his emotions come to the surface. Lying on his bed, his eyes slowly closed and he fell asleep. He awoke with a start; it was light and he had no idea of the time. He reached for his travelling alarm clock. It was only half-past six so he lay back on his bed feeling a great deal better. As his head cleared, however, visions of the previous evening came back to him, although the effect was not as dramatic as it had been.

Looking round his room he realised that he had to get himself back into the land of the living. His cases needed to be packed and everything had to be made ready for his return to England. He looked in the mirror in the bathroom and could see a mark around his neck starting to show. It had changed from bright red to a dull reddish blue. As he packed his case and sorted through his clothes, he found what he was looking for, a roll neck sweater.

Showered and dressed, he made his way out of the hotel in search of breakfast. He didn't want to eat in the hotel as he still needed some time alone to collect his thoughts. The remainder of the morning went quickly and he was now almost ready to go.

Georges knocked on Ben's door at midday and was pleased to find his friend in a lot better shape than when he had left him the previous evening.

'Comment ca va?'

'Très bien, et tu?'

'I'm ok, is nice to see you looking better.'

Ben looked at his friend warmly. 'Merci, Georges, you have helped me so much, you and your brother.'

'We are all brothers and we help each other.'

Impulsively they both put their arms around each other, knowing theirs was a friendship that would last a lifetime.

'Georges, I have left something for you in my room – perhaps you will remember me when you use it.' He pointed to the record player, which brought a broad grin to Georges' face.

'Ah, thank you!'

Sunday slipped by and Ben felt that he was as ready as he could be. He had a comparatively good night and felt pleasantly refreshed as he waited for his taxi. It was a very nice surprise when Georges appeared at the hotel entrance with Odette. She approached Ben with open arms and kissed him on the cheek.

'We could not let you go without saying farewell.'

Ben had a strange sense of embarrassment mixed with regret at leaving his friends.

Odette continued to hold his hand. 'We will miss you. Who can teach me English now you are leaving us?'

'Your English is better than mine anyway and I am sure you and Georges will be able to teach each other,' Ben joked.

As the taxi drew up in front of the hotel, Odette gave Ben a final kiss on the cheek and Georges shook his hand and placed his arm round Ben's shoulder.

'Au revoir.' Ben's voice shook a little.

'No, no it is à bientôt. We will see you soon – if not here, we will come to England!'

Ben could see tears start to well up in Odette's eyes. He grabbed his cases and made his way to the taxi, then turned and gave them a small wave as he got in. He watched them waving back until they were out of sight. They had been a part of his life that would have an influence on whatever he did in years to come.

22

A t the station, Ben cast his mind back, remembering when he first arrived, and thought of how much he had learnt. He had made good friends and seen horrendous things, and now he was going home. His journey was uneventful and he made it from Gare du Nord to Gare de l'Est without taking his mind off his journey. He did not think about his last visit and was determined to put it to the back of his mind. A wave of relief flooded over him as the train pulled out of the station. Calais came and he was focused on just wanting to get home. On board the ferry he sat in the lounge and did something he had never done before – he ordered a coffee noir and a brandy. He sipped the coffee and brandy alternatively and was soon feeling much better than he had in the last three days. He went up on deck to watch the white cliffs appear, and as he went towards the rail he thought of Sophie and how much he wanted to see her. It wouldn't be long!

Treading on English soil again made him smile, and customs and passport control were easy. The final leg was the train to London, and as Ben got into a carriage with his cases, the smell of tobacco and musty seats seemed comforting in a way. The train was fairly full and passengers came and went as they neared London, some ending their journeys and others starting.

Ben watched as the fields changed into housing and he knew that the train was nearing its final destination. Waterloo swallowed the train and Ben made ready to get off with his suitcases. He struggled through the door and onto the platform. Looking up, he could see the platform clock showing 7:30pm, and although it was still light Ben could feel the chill of evening approaching.

Getting a taxi was easy. Ben had already changed some of his money into sterling on the ferry and anything left he would sort out at the bank. He had enough funds to get him home. Clambering out of the taxi with his luggage, he made his way to the front door of his uncle's house and nervously rang the doorbell. He could hear footsteps approaching and the door opened; his aunt stood in the doorway.

She threw her arms around him. 'You're a sight for sore eyes.' Her voice was emotional and trembled a little.

'It's good to see you, too,' Ben said grinning as he grabbed her and lifted her off her feet.

'Put me down, you don't know your own strength.'

Ben picked up his cases and followed her into the house.

'What do you want to do, get unpacked or have a cup of tea and something to eat?'

'To be honest, I want to get these suitcases sorted out first and then I can relax.'

'You get yourself organised and I'll put the kettle on.'

He took his cases up the stairs. Everything about the house hit him – the smell of furniture polish mixed with the scent of freshly cut flowers, the tread of the carpet on the stairs, the feel of the banister – it was so good to be home. His room was just as he had left it.

'Home,' he said to himself. 'I'm home.'

After unpacking he went downstairs and into the kitchen where his aunt was making tea. 'It's so good to be home, Aunt

Sarah, I didn't realise just how much I've missed it.'

'Well, you're back now and we don't want you going off again.' Sarah turned to look at her nephew. He had grown taller and may have put on a few pounds here and there. His face though seemed to have lines where none existed before.

'Come and sit down and tell me everything that's happened since we last saw you.'

Ben felt a shudder, as if someone had walked over his grave. He knew he would never tell any member of his family what had really happened, unless he had no other option. The day had been successful, he had achieved what he wanted, he had reached home without incident, his sense of place had returned and he felt comfortable and relaxed. He slept well without the troublesome dreams that had disturbed him over the last few nights.

The morning was bright and Ben looked around his room from his bed; it felt so good to be home. As he stretched his neck he felt a little stiff, but the soreness had gone. He looked in the mirror and saw that the mark from his attack remained but was more of a long bruise. Getting dressed, he carefully selected another roll neck jumper just to avoid awkward questions, and a pair of clean jeans. He was surprised to see his uncle at the breakfast table.

'Hello, here comes the prodigal son.' Steven stood and put his arms round Ben's shoulders. 'I think you've put on a bit of weight and grown a few inches. What have the French been feeding you on?'

Ben's face broke into a broad smile. 'It's all the butter and cream they use, and of course the croissants and cakes don't help'.

'It's great to have you back, Ben.'

Over breakfast Ben and his uncle discussed all that had

happened in France as well as what Steven had been doing in England – his business venture into transportation. Ben looked at his watch then at Steven.

'It's ok, Ben, I've taken the day off so I'm in no hurry to go anywhere.'

Sarah wagged her finger at him. 'Now don't you monopolise the boy. You know that Sophie is probably on her way here now so let him get prepared because she is going to be firing questions at him left right and centre.'

Steven tapped Ben on the shoulder, repeated 'Good to have you back,' and headed towards the kitchen door saying that he had some things to do in the garden.

'Are you feeling the cold?' Sarah asked Ben.

'Not really, why do you ask?'

'It's just that wearing a roll neck at this time of year seems a little odd.' Ben's mind went into overdrive. He had to come up with something fairly convincing, not only for his aunt but also for anyone else who might ask about the marks on his neck.

'I had an accident a few days ago in the hotel. It was my own fault, I wasn't looking where I was going and ran into a washing line at the back of the hotel. It sort of wrapped itself round my neck and gave me quite a turn.' Ben thought *now or never* and pulled the sweater down to reveal the mark on his neck.

'Oh, Ben, that must have hurt, it looks bad. Did you see a doctor?' His aunt's face was full of concern.

'It's not as bad as it looks and the bruising should be gone in a few days.'

'Well, if you think its ok, fine, but I don't know what Sophie will say.'

Just then his uncle appeared at the door. 'What Sophie will say about what?' he asked

'Look at this.' Sarah pointed to the mark on Ben's neck.

'Ouch, I bet that was sore.' Steven winced.

'I'm ok, honestly,' Ben said as he adjusted the sweater.

He changed the subject and told them he was expected back at the hotel on Thursday and needed to be ready to start a new job in the kitchen. When asked what sort of role he said he didn't know and that David Burdett would tell him when he met him on Thursday morning.

Steven's voice became more serious as he told Ben that they needed to speak later about what they were going to do with his family house. Steven had been looking after it as part of his own portfolio of rented properties, but as Ben was coming up to twenty-one, his trust fund would soon become available and plans needed to be made.

'Would it be ok to talk about that after Sophie's been?'

'Some time later this week would be fine, Ben. It's just that we need to think about your future.'

Ben had forgotten about his trust fund and the income from the rental of his parents' house that had been accumulating.

The doorbell rang and Ben jumped up; he didn't have to be told it would be Sophie at the door. He pulled the door open and didn't have time to breathe before Sophie had her arms around his neck and planted a massive kiss on his lips. She was like a limpet and he thought she would never let go, but she had to draw breath at some stage. She released him slowly, and stepping back looked at him as if she was planning to eat him.

'Ben Croxley, don't you ever leave me again.'

'I won't, I promise.'

As if she wanted to hold him to that promise, she grabbed his arm tightly as they walked into the house.

The four of them sat around the kitchen table. 'I think

another cup of something might be in order, that's if Sophie can let go of Ben for long enough,' his aunt said as she made her way towards the kettle.

Ben went through everything again for Sophie. He didn't mind, and his aunt and uncle sat and listened to the question-and-answer session that Sophie put Ben through. It wasn't until their conversation came to a natural break that Sarah mentioned Ben's accident and Sophie gently pulled the collar of Ben's sweater down revealing the bruising on his neck.

'Oh, Ben, that looks nasty.' Sophie ran her finger lightly over the bruise.

'That's exactly what I said,' Sarah agreed.

'Does it hurt?'

'No, it's ok now.' Ben had to go through his story again for Sophie, who kept hold of Ben's hand as he spoke.

Then it was her turn, and once Sophie started telling Ben how she had got on during his absence, there was no stopping her. Ben listened and smiled at how deeply involved and knowledgeable about the day-to-day management of the hotel she had become.

While Ben had been in France, Sophie had really progressed with her course at college and had gained so much confidence working with Annabel Stewart that she now felt able to run reception on her own. Her relationship with her dad had been put under strain when she tried to run the flat, do her job, and also her course work all at the same time, but they had coped, and remained not only father and daughter but the best of friends.

'You know I told you about the policeman and Annabel,' Sophie turned to Ben, 'well, that's been going on for some time now and I think it's getting serious.'

'Hotel gossip, you can't beat it for drama,' Ben smiled.

The following few days were going to be busy for Ben. He would be seeing Burdett in a couple of days to find out what position he would be offered, and he needed to have a chat with his uncle. Sophie told Ben that his aunt, with a little help from her, had arranged a small get-together for the weekend. She went through what they had planned.

'That's great. I don't start work proper until Monday.'

'We shall be in the garden and have cool refreshing drinks. The food will be arranged by your aunt and me, so I don't want any complaints!' She laughed in the way that Ben loved.

Time slipped by faster than expected. Ben had spoken to his uncle about the trust fund. It appeared that the income from the house had been substantial and a tidy sum had built up. Steven suggested that Ben might continue with the arrangement for the time being. 'We have decimalisation arriving next year and god knows what effect that is going to have on our lives.'

Ben had forgotten about the forthcoming changes; his life had been so tied up with everything French that what was happening in England had somehow passed him by.

'I have a feeling that things are going to become more expensive and if the government doesn't control the financial stability of the country, things could implode,' Steven continued.

Ben looked at the concern on his uncle's face. 'I'm very happy to keep things as they are, if you are happy to keep managing the house as part of your business.' Ben trusted him totally and felt relieved that his uncle would stay in charge.

The get-together at the weekend went well. Sophie brought her dad, which was the first time he had met Ben's aunt and uncle. They got on well. His uncle could talk to anyone about anything and his aunt was her usual good-natured self, full of curiosity. It had been a glorious day; the sun shone and people smiled and laughed and Ben, looking round at the faces in the garden, concluded it was all good, in fact better than good.

One decision Ben had to make was how to get to work. Would he get his bike out of the garden shed or would he commute by tube? He had noticed that, since returning, when he blew his nose, a black deposit ended up on his handkerchief, unlike in Rheims where the pollution was negligible. He decided that for the sake of his health he would take the underground and join the thousands of others squeezed into a tin can and shot through a tunnel. He recognised that he was not as fit as he had been and that cycling six miles a day might prove a little taxing. It might be an idea to speak to his uncle about the possibility of driving lessons.

The next day, as Ben walked into the kitchen entrance of the hotel, he had mixed feelings – nerves, together with a certain amount of excitement. It was the smells that hit him first. He had always found them comforting. He changed into his whites and made his way to David Burdett's office.

He knocked on the door and heard Burdett's 'Come in.'

As he opened the door his boss got to his feet and moved quickly round his desk. 'My god, there's a sight for sore eyes. Come in, Ben, grab a chair.'

Burdett studied him as he seated himself and saw a young man who had matured during his time in France. A little older and hopefully a lot wiser, he thought. 'I spoke to Craig Hinson yesterday and had a long chat regarding what to do with you.'

'I hope nothing bad?'

'No, on the contrary he was most complimentary.'

Burdett explained to Ben that Mark, his current sous chef at the Rosegarth, had been offered the chance to go into business with a partner. They were in the initial stages of buying a small restaurant in Leeds. Ben remembered that was where Mark came from. 'It won't be happening for at least two months and my thinking is that you could shadow Mark until he leaves and then, if you are up to the job, take over from him when he leaves.'

Ben was over the moon. If he could secure a sous chef post his future looked pretty good.

'What do you think? Would you like a little time to consider your options?' Burdett asked.

Ben jumped in straightaway. 'It would be another great opportunity for me and I would be an idiot if I said no to it!'

David Burdett sat back in his chair, satisfied, and said to Ben to tell him all about France. They sat in Burdett's office for about an hour and Ben went through all the jobs he had been given and how he liked some more than others. He praised the organisation of Craig Hinson and also told Burdett of his kindness in inviting him to his home. Their conversation came to an end and Burdett stood, opened his office door and called for Mark to join them. At the end of their discussion, all parties were happy and Mark took Ben off to start the next phase of his career.

23

Annabel Stewart had taken Sophie under her wing, not in a protective way but as a possible assistant or even deputy. They worked well together, and although Sophie needed her confidence building, Annabel could see potential in the way she approached the job and she was not shy of work. The way Sophie dealt with guests was good to see. She could use her carefully practised look of innocence to get most men on her side without too much trouble. Her skill in maintaining the ledgers and registers was exceptional and her handwriting was far better than Annabel's.

Annabel judged it would be some time before Sophie would be ready to run a hotel but she was ready and willing for her to stand in for herself. So far, Sophie had only been left in charge for no longer than a day. However, it was clear to all those who worked with her that it wouldn't be long before she was running the show.

Sophie raised her head from the register as she felt the presence of someone at the desk. 'Oh, hello, it's Mr Russell, isn't it?'

Peter didn't feel in the mood to correct anyone about his title; Mr would do just nicely. Sophie smiled her usual welcoming smile.

'Yes, is Ms Stewart available?'

Sophie knew that Annabel wouldn't really like that form of address – she always insisted on being called Annabel, no Mrs, Miss or Ms, just Annabel.

'I'll just go and see.'

The door to the office was closed. Sophie knew that her boss was in the middle of sorting rooms out for the following week. She poked her head round the door. 'It's that nice policeman to see you.' Annabel looked up and winked at Sophie.

'Tell him I won't be a minute, if he'd like to take a seat.'

Sophie passed the message on and Peter Russell found a comfortable seat and picked up a newspaper. Not long after, Annabel stepped out from her office, smoothing her skirt as she came round into the main reception area. Peter looked at her and thought how attractive she was, then inwardly cursed himself. Surely he was big enough and old enough to be able to control his thoughts every time she came into his sight. He stood up to greet her. It had become a ritual when they met, trying to decide how to greet each other; a handshake? a kiss on the cheek? or just hello? He felt like a nervous teenager. She held out her hand and as he shook it, she did something for the first time – she leant forward and kissed him on the cheek.

'Hello,' she said, in a low voice that made Peter nervous. 'Would you like coffee?'

He almost stuttered but regained his self-composure. 'Yes please, I haven't had a coffee all day.'

She led the way into the restaurant and they walked to a table near to the kitchen. There were no guests, it being far too early. A waiter popped his head round the door and Annabel asked for two coffees, both with milk but no sugar.

'You remembered,' Peter said as he pulled the chair out for her to sit down.

'Oh yes, I've got a good memory for what our customers want.'

She knows just what to say to wind me up, Peter thought.

'What brings you to our humble establishment today?'

'Something good and something bad.'

'That doesn't sound promising.' Her response was light.

'The bad thing is that I have to ask if we could rearrange our dinner date – I'm being sent to Paris that weekend so I won't be able to make it.'

'Paris indeed.' Annabel became more attentive. 'When are you going and for how long?'

'It's only for three days. Basically, I fly out on Thursday morning and return on the Saturday evening.'

'It's still Paris, Peter. Just think what I could do in Paris. I need a new outfit. It would be heavenly.' She lowered her voice and slid closer to him. 'How big is your suitcase, Peter, do you have room for a little one?'

He thought to himself, *this time I'm going to call your bluff, Annabel.* 'My suitcase is large enough and I'm sure I could squeeze you in.'

To his utter surprise she told him to wait a minute, dashed back to her office and returned with her large diary.

'What are the dates again?'

He was flummoxed for a moment. 'Oh,' he said, and gave her the dates.

She leafed through her diary, glanced at him, and smiled coyly. 'That should be no problem. Which airline are you flying with and where will you be staying?'

Things were going a little too fast for Peter so he tried to slow things down. 'But you can't just take time off like that, can you?'

'I'm the boss – so everyone keeps telling me – so I can.'

'What about hotels and flights and things?'

She could see he was getting hot under the collar. 'Peter, I am in the leisure industry and have contacts all over the world. If I can't arrange a three-day trip to Paris then I am not worth my salt. Leave me the details and I will phone you later to tell you how I get on.'

Peter's mind was working overtime. What, how, and when could this be sorted out? He was going on police business, not on a holiday weekend. He would have to clear it with his boss. Or would he? She was a private individual travelling to Paris for a weekend break and it just so happened that they would be going at the same time. Anyway, it was early days yet. Despite what she said, she might not be able to get a flight or hotel accommodation. He would wait and see. They finished their coffee. Annabel said she had to dash, things to organise. As she turned to go back to the reception, she blew him a kiss. The restaurant was still empty but even so he felt redness creeping up his face.

Annabel was thinking to herself that she would not let this chance to cement her relationship with Peter Russell pass. In her office she picked up the phone and started to make calls. Her contacts were very helpful and she managed to get on the same flight as Peter and, eventually, after a bit of favour calling, she successfully reserved a room in the same hotel. Sitting back in her chair she smiled. 'I've got you now, Mr Russell!'

Peter got his team together and explained to them that he was going to Paris for a meeting with the Police Nationale. He would be speaking to members of the Central Directorate of Judicial Police who were responsible for serious crime, and to help him he needed the most up-to-date information they had on anyone linked to the drugs operation in their patch. His main reason for going was that the description of the 'bodyguard' that had been given by David Burdett and Ben Croxley matched a body found in a rather seedy part of Paris. The French police were mystified as there was no physical evidence as to who the man was. He had been well dressed and appeared to be in good condition, but what he was doing and how he had ended up in a region of Paris that was not usually frequented by those who could do otherwise, was very odd.

'So, gentlemen, get everything you have on the case and let me have it by close of play on Wednesday.'

His team went back to their desks and started to assemble all the data they had on the case.

It was around three in the afternoon that Peter Russell's phone rang. He immediately recognised Annabel's voice.

'Peter, it looks like you may have company on your trip.'

Peter drew a deep breath. 'Have you managed to get a flight, then?'

'Not only a flight, but I have a room in the same hotel. Do you know your room number?' This was getting very serious.

'I've got the room number somewhere but I don't know it off the top of my head.'

'No matter, we shall see how close we are when we get there.'

This was going to be difficult. He decided he would run it by his boss, just to be on the safe side.

'Do you want me to pick you up on Thursday, or will you make your own way to Heathrow?'

'Could you pick me up, say about four o'clock? That will give us time to get to the airport and perhaps for me a quick look at the perfume counters.'

This now looked very bad! Exploring perfume counters was not his style at all. Still, he was prepared to go with the flow.

'Annabel, we always meet in the hotel so give me your address and I'll be with you at four.'

The address given, a look of satisfaction passed over her face as she leaned back and thought of what she would buy.

In the kitchen of the Rosegarth, Ben was finding his feet again. He had made contact with his friend Rodger, who was now a fully-fledged chef de partie at the hotel. They had long conversations as they were carrying out their various tasks, Rodger of course being full of questions relating to 'French girls' and what were they like. Ben humoured him by relating the story of his close encounter with Gabrielle and how the poor young commis chef got his nose broken. Other than that, it was general chat about life in France and did Ben think Rodger would like it? He was also a good source of gossip in the kitchen. He knew everyone and their business, so was able to fill Ben in on all that was going on, and Ben found it very useful to get up-to-date.

Feeling confident to take on the role that Burdett had suggested to him, he shadowed Mark throughout the day and found him to be a first-class tutor. His way with the staff was similar to Ben's, which gained him a fair degree of respect. Ben became aware that the role of sous chef was full of challenges, and he watched as Mark planned the tasks for each member of the brigade and directed work at the various stations to achieve the desired result.

The part of the job he found the most rewarding was working closely with the head chef as he planned menus. Carrying out inventories of produce and their purchase was not so exciting but it was all part of the job. He found that his time in France had made him even more hygiene conscious than before he left, and he would regularly make sure that each station was cleaned down properly and remind chefs de partie and commis chefs that all their heads would be on the block if any customer, or member of staff for that matter, fell ill with food poisoning.

Ben had been getting to know Sophie again after being apart for such a long time and was thinking of their future together. She on the other hand, had been fully engrossed in her job and was anxious when Annabel said she wanted a private chat.

'I have decided to take a weekend off – well, more like a couple of days. I shall be away from Thursday night to Sunday morning. So, young lady, I have decided to leave the running of reception in your hands. Do you think you can handle that?'

Sophie looked at Annabel in surprise and shuffled in her chair. 'Erm, yes, I think so.'

Annabel could see some hesitation in Sophie's response. 'You will be surrounded by people you know, and if you have any questions or doubts, you can ask them.' She went through the names and positions of those Sophie would be able to call upon if she needed to. 'Most importantly I have asked our night manager, Harvey Cooper, to be on call over the period so he will be your first stop.'

Sophie was aware that normally the night manager would have simply changed to a day shift and covered for Annabel, but this was her big chance to show that she could run reception.

'You will also have Deborah from the restaurant to help you as you did when you first came to work on reception. I have had a word with her and made it very clear that you are in charge and it will be up to you to resolve any problems that may arise. Are you ok with that?'

Sophie said she was perfectly happy (delighted in fact, though she kept that to herself) and would not let Annabel down.

Annabel was satisfied that all eventualities were covered, and on Thursday at two pm she left the hotel, went home to gather her luggage and wait for Peter Russell to pick her up.

Before Peter was able to get off on his trip, a knock sounded on his office door and Ian Bedford's head appeared.

'Do you have a minute?' It was less a question than an order.

'Yes, of course, please sit down.' Ian Bedford settled his long frame into a comfortable chair.

'I've come down to see how your trip to Paris is working out.'

This was an opportunity to broach the subject of Annabel, but Peter decided he'd better run through his plan first.

'I have all the latest material here,' he held up a green file, 'and any other last-minute things the boys are going to brief me about before I leave.'

Bedford opened the file and skimmed through it without really studying anything in particular. 'Do you know exactly who will be at the meeting?'

'Yes, I've been sent an agenda and a list of those attending – it's in the front of the file.' Peter reached over and opened the flap in the front cover.

Bedford frowned and this time took more of an interest. 'Not many, then, just you two members of the French police team and someone from Interpol. Do you think that's adequate?'

Peter nodded his head. 'Yes. As long as they have the information we need, it should be ok.'

Bedford started to rise from his chair saying that he thought all was going well, when Peter said he had one more thing to get Bedford's advice on.

'Oh yes, and what's that?'

Peter cleared his throat. 'It's personal and I just wanted to clear it with you. I have a friend who will be visiting Paris at the same time as me and it may be possible that our paths cross. Would you have any objection to that?'

'May I ask who this person is?'

'That's the other difficulty. She has been mentioned in a current case.'

'Who is it?' he asked again.

'It's Annabel Stewart from the Rosegarth.'

Ian Bedford sat back down. 'Let me tell you a little about Annabel Stewart.'

Peter was taken aback. What did his Commander know about her?

Bedford frowned for a moment then began to tell Peter as much as he was able to.

'Peter, there are several hotels in the London area that are used to accommodate visiting dignitaries and members of foreign governments. These hotels are a valuable asset to certain government departments. Rosegarth is one of those hotels and Miss Stewart is, shall we say, in a position to acquire certain information that may be of use to the departments involved.'

Peter looked utterly gob smacked. 'Are you telling me that Annabel works for one of those departments?'

'That's not for me to confirm or otherwise. I just wanted you to know we are on the same side, so I don't think that you spending some time with Miss Stewart in Paris would jeopardise our relationship with any other government departments. Please have fun, if that's what you intend to do.' With that bombshell and his slightly ambiguous remark, Ian Bedford got up and left the office. For a few minutes, Peter just sat feeling totally bemused.

Peter drew up outside the address Annabel had given him. It

was a block of very smart flats which Peter thought must cost an arm and a leg. Before he had time to press the intercom bell, Annabel stepped out of the lift. The concierge helped her with her suitcase to the door. *My god,* Peter thought, *who needs that amount of luggage for just two days?* He took the case from the porter and loaded it into the boot. He went to open the door for her but she beat him to it.

'I might be a weak and feeble woman, but I can open a car door, Peter. But thank you.'

The drive to Heathrow didn't take long; Peter had driven to the airport many times before. As he drove, he told Annabel that he had a bone to pick with her and it might take all the time they had in Paris for her to explain. Her response was to lean over and plant a kiss on his cheek.

24

Their flight to Paris was uneventful, Peter had not flown all that often and still got a childish thrill. For Annabel it was just another means of getting from one place to another. They arrived at their hotel in the early evening; amusingly, Peter had a single room at the hotel and Annabel a double. *This could prove interesting*, she thought. After they had unpacked, they met for drinks. Annabel had with her a map of Paris that she picked up at the reception.

'Now where shall we eat tonight?' Annabel was determined to make this visit one that they would both enjoy.

'I have no idea,' Peter said, 'I was lost as soon as we left the plane.'

Annabel looked at the map. 'Are you prepared to leave the decision-making to a mere woman?'

Peter laughed. She knew just how to lighten a conversation. 'I shall place myself entirely in your hands, and will follow your instructions implicitly.'

They enjoyed their evening but it became awkward when they returned to the hotel.

'What's your room like, Peter?'

'A bit pokey, but it will do. What about yours?'

'Very nice, thank you. Would you like to see it? Perhaps a night cap?'

Peter followed her into her spacious room, which had a sofa, and a desk and chair in front a large window. She opened the mini bar and started looking at its contents. 'What would you like – we appear to have scotch, brandy, beer, and something that looks very potent.'

'Scotch and soda, please.'

He sat on the sofa and watched as she moved around the room, her dress swaying with the movement of her hips as she brought the drinks and placed them on the table in front of the sofa. She sat next to him, kicking off her shoes and stretching. As she did her body arched slightly and he could see just what a handful she could be.

'Have you enjoyed yourself?' she asked as her finger traced the edge of her glass. She moved closer to him and as their bodies touched, he could feel the heat of her thighs as she pressed them against his.

'I have had a night I shall remember.'

She smiled provocatively and said, 'It isn't over yet, Peter.'

She took his glass and placed it on the table; looking into his eyes she leaned forward and kissed him. She parted her lips slightly and her tongue touched his lips. As she loosened his tie, he reached for her zip and began to slowly draw it down. She stepped out of her dress; her cream silk slip hugged the contours of her body in all the right places. She expertly removed Peter's shirt, kissing him again. He picked her up and carried her to the bed, where they drew slowly together, passion starting to rise as his lips traced the line of her neck, and as their bodies met, they became lost in each other.

In the morning they both left Annabel's room and headed for breakfast.

'My meeting is set for nine-thirty and I need to find my way to the offices of the DCPJ, Peter said anxiously.'

Annabel stretched a hand across the table, placing it delicately on Peter's. 'I think it might be a good idea to get a taxi – finding your way across Paris by metro at this time of day might give you problems.'

Peter nodded. He looked at her. She was beautiful, and if he could see her across the breakfast table every morning, he would be a happy man.

Annabel checked her handbag. 'I shall be going into every shop I can find and I shall be spending a great deal of money. 'When in Paris', as they say!'

'I think it's 'when in Rome',' Peter murmured.

They finished their breakfast and he left by taxi for his meeting while she opened her map and decided to head for the Faubourg Saint-Honoré district which she knew had some of the world's top fashion establishments.

Peter's taxi dropped him at the offices of the Central Directorate of the Judicial Police and he managed to reach the office of la brigade des stupéfiants – the French equivalent of the drugs squad – commonly referred to as les Stups. His meeting took place in a small room with only himself, two members of the French police and a very smart looking representative from Interpol. The Frenchmen wanted to know everything Peter had on the drugs situation in London and were also keen to know about the situation in the rest of the country, so the meeting took some time.

It took Peter some fierce concentration to keep focused on the case in hand. He was very glad of the guy from Interpol, otherwise the language barrier would have made the whole meeting almost impossible. One of the items was to discuss a killing that had happened some time ago in a Paris suburb. This was particularly interesting on account of the description of a man wanted for questioning by the British Police that had been circulated by Interpol, which matched that of the dead man. Peter was impressed by the information the French had been able to gather on this man. He told them that when back in England, he would return to the two people who had given the description and see if they recognised the photograph.

He left the meeting feeling that he had accomplished what he had set out to do. He had the names and contact numbers of his French counterparts and that of the guy from Interpol. He placed the photo of the dead man in his file and made ready to leave. He also made a mental note that when he got back to the UK he would make sure he took whatever course was necessary to improve his French to a level that would make life a lot easier in future.

They had worked their way through lunch, just having sandwiches and Perrier, and now Peter was ready for something to eat and perhaps a drink or two to celebrate the success of his visit. He wondered how Annabel had got on with her shopping.

He soon found out. She struggled into the lift, very pleased with her purchases – an armful of bags bearing designer names boldly displayed. Knowing they only had that one evening, she was determined to make the most of it. She had taken a risk and booked a table at Le Cinq, one of the restaurants in the George Cinq hotel. She intended it to be a night to remember.

Peter's room stood empty as he seemed to have taken up residence in Annabel's. She told Peter he needed to go to his room to change as he had to look smart for a surprise she had arranged. Nervously he knocked on her door later on and could not believe the sight that stood in front of him. Annabel looked amazing. She was wearing the most gorgeous cocktail dress that enhanced her figure and enriched the colour of her hair and eyes. Peter had difficulty in taking his eyes off her.

'You like?' she pouted, pirouetting coquettishly.

'Oh I like,' he grinned.

She led the way and stayed in the lead all evening. Her French being far better than Peter's, he graciously let her do most of the ordering. What a night they had. Both enjoyed the grandeur of the restaurant and the sumptuousness of the food.

In the taxi on their way back to the hotel, Peter just couldn't find the words. He gently pressed his lips on hers. 'Tonight will live with me for a long time, thank you so much.'

*

Sophie, meanwhile, studied the bookings and decided that, with Deborah's help, she had managed to hold her own and keep on top of things. Guests had been coming and going, and there had been no major upsets, which pleased her. However, she felt that, due to putting herself under pressure by trying to imagine what could go wrong, she had been a little short with Ben at times. Thinking about him, she realised that since his return, Ben had seemed preoccupied with something. Sophie had asked him if there was anything bothering him but he would only say it was down to his return to the hotel and the added responsibility he was trying to get used to.

Sophie felt so much better when she saw Annabel walking through the hotel lobby on the Sunday morning. She had made sure she would be there to welcome her back and tell her how things had gone in her absence. Annabel looked around the foyer and could see no signs of major disaster. Sophie popped up from behind the reception desk, which made Annabel think of a jack-in-the-box. She smiled warmly at her.

'Hello, and how did you get on without me?'

Sophie looked very serious. 'We did very well. All the bookings have been registered correctly and the guests had no complaints on leaving.'

'That's good to hear.' Annabel could see that Sophie was anxious to please. 'Tell me everything that's happened.'

Sophie followed Annabel into her office. The two women went through the various registers and till receipts; everything balanced and everything looked in order.

'Well, I guess I shall have to go away more often.' Annabel turned to see a slight blush come to Sophie's cheeks. 'Thank you, Sophie, and how did you get on with Deborah?'

'We were fine and liked working together. We shared the duties and things got done on time without any mistakes and we enjoyed having the responsibility.'

'Has Deborah returned to her job in the restaurant?'

Sophie said that she had taken two days off before starting back, and although she had had to work over the weekend said she would like to do it more often.

'It looks like you have a partner in crime, which can only be good for me.' Annabel was pleased.

*

Peter Russell returned to his office on the Monday morning with something of a mind-blowing piece of information. He went straight to Ian Bedford's office. Bedford's secretary, Margaret, sat at her desk with the telephone receiver to her ear. 'I have just been trying to get you on the phone.'

'I'm here now, what –?'

'Mr Bedford wants to speak to you as early as possible.'

'That's good, because I need to speak to him.'

She reached towards the intercom, and pressed one of the many buttons.

A voice echoed from the voice box. 'Yes, Margaret?'

'I have Peter Russell wanting to have a word.'

'Good, send him in.'

Peter knocked and went in.

'I hope you have plenty of interesting news for me, Peter.'

Peter pulled up a chair and started to go through the events of the previous week. He spoke of his meeting and how he had managed to get contact details for both the French police and Interpol. Placing his folder on the desk, he opened it and took out a photograph which he passed to Bedford.

'This is a picture of a murder victim who met his end in one of the seedier parts of Paris.'

Bedford took the photo and studied it. 'So what has that to do with us?

'If you remember, we circulated a description of the person who acted as waiter cum bodyguard in the meeting at Steyning's house the night before he died. The French police thought that the match with this corpse was too good not to follow it up.'

'I can see what you mean. Did they have any further intel on the deceased?'

'Something rather intriguing came to light. Our witnesses thought that this particular individual was some sort of American ex-military type, but what Interpol discovered was that his origins were far from American.'

Bedford read Peter's report more carefully, then closed the file and pushed it towards Peter. 'How are you going to use this?'

'This is the only clue they have at the moment and I need confirmation that this was the guy our chefs saw in Steyning's house that night. My next step is to go to the Rosegarth and speak to them.'

'Fine go ahead, but just before you shoot off, I want to get a couple of copies of that photograph. Margaret, can you come in, please.'

She entered the room in her ever-efficient manner and he asked her to get two copies of the photograph. He needed them urgently, he said, and she should use his name if she had any bother. Taking the photograph, Margaret hurried from the room.

'With a bit of luck, we should get the copies back within the hour. I'll give you a ring when they're here. Something that will interest you, by the way – the forensic lab has been able to identify the stuff used by Steyning that caused his death. It appears that a substance has been developed that is a great deal stronger than heroin. It can appear the same, but if a user were to get it confused with their usual fix, it could be fatal. We think this was the case with Steyning. This new drug is cheaper to produce, apparently, and once widely available not only will it massively increase the profits of the producers and dealers but be far easier to distribute. What needs to be established is whether Steyning took the drug knowingly, or was given it as heroin.

As regards the situation as a whole, we need to find out where this drug is coming from and who is organising its distribution. Our American friends know the drug as 'fentanyl' and they tell me it's a synthetic opioid similar to morphine, but fifty to a hundred times more potent. It comes in many forms – powder – dropped onto blotting paper – put into eye droppers, and sometimes in pill form that looks a lot like other hard drugs. Sometimes it's mixed with other drugs, but the most concerning factor of all is that it's cheap. So you see, Peter, this is a matter of urgency. We have to get this under control and if possible stop it altogether. If you manage to get any further information regarding this drug or who is handling it, make sure it gets to the right people.'

With that bombshell Ian Bedford sat back in his chair. Peter realised that the meeting had reached an end and got up to leave.

'I hope your journey to Paris had more than success from a work point of view.' He smiled at Peter with a knowing look.

Bedford didn't have to wait long. Margaret soon brought the copies of the photos back to him. 'Make sure the original is given back to Peter Russell, please, Margaret.'

Peter was glad to get the photo back. He studied it closely and tried to make sense of the other information he had brought back from Paris. His next move wasn't to go straight to the Rosegarth, however. First he needed to brief his team on the latest developments and find out what they had been up to in his absence.

After briefing his team, Peter set out for the Rosegarth. He wanted to crack on with this case and hoped he could make some headway after speaking to the two chefs; unless that was just wishful thinking. Peter decided to take Chris Stamford with him. Their conversation as they drove to the hotel centred mainly on Peter's trip to Paris, although of course there was no mention of Annabel. At the hotel they were greeted by Sophie, who immediately asked if they wanted to see Annabel. She was very surprised when Peter Russell told her that his business today was with the chefs.

'I'll see if I can get hold of Mr Burdett,' she said and lifted the telephone receiver. There was a brief conversation. 'Mr Burdett will be with you in a moment. Would you like to take a seat?'

'No, it's ok, we'll be alright on our feet.'

Chris Stamford looked a little aggrieved at this as his feet were killing him after a terrible game of rugby the night before, but he thought he'd better do as his boss said.

David Burdett collected them from reception and led them to his office. When they had settled down, Peter asked David if he could get young Ben to join them. Burdett put his head round the door and asked one of the commis chefs to fetch Ben. They chatted about the hotel until he arrived.

'Hello, Ben.' Peter held out his hand. Ben grasped it and took a seat. Burdett asked Russell why he had asked to see them.

'There has been a development in the Steyning case and I need your help with something.'

'Anything we can help with, please ask.'

Peter opened his brief case and took out a folder. 'I have just returned from Paris where my colleagues in the French police told me of a suspicious death in a rather dubious part of their city.' Peter explained how they needed help in identifying the dead man. 'I have a photograph that I want you to have a look at. It's not pleasant because it was taken post-mortem, so prepare yourselves.' He passed the photo to Burdett who looked at it and grimaced; it was definitely not a photo you would show your mother.

'Do you recognise this man?' Burdett said he did and passed it to Ben. The blood from Ben's face drained immediately he saw the face and he turned white.

'Are you ok, Ben?' Russell asked. Ben gulped down a mouthful of air,

'Yes, I'm alright, but it's not very nice, is it?'

Russell said that he was sorry about the picture, but did Ben recognise him? Ben nodded his head. 'Yes. He's the man that was at Steyning's dinner party, the one that acted as a sort of waiter or man servant.'

Burdett again said, 'We thought he was American, possibly an ex-soldier, but we weren't sure.'

'That's very interesting, because our friends in the French police and Interpol have discovered that although he may have spoken like an American, dressed like an American, and probably walked like an American, in fact he was born in the Soviet Union.'

'A Russian!' Burdett was amazed.

'Well, yes, at least a citizen of the Soviet Bloc,' Russell replied.

Ben was still suffering from seeing the photo. He had a vision of the scene in Paris with the blood pumping from the dead man's neck. He started to shake and had difficulty in controlling his hands.

'Are you sure you're alright, Ben?' Burdett's concern was fatherly.

'Yes, I'll be ok, it's just – well, seeing that –' he pointed to the photo of the dead man.

'Russian, you say. Do you know what he was doing here?' Burdett asked.

'Not yet, but we do have a name, for all the good that will do us. He was born Fedyenka Balabanov. Which is a mouthful in itself. More than that we have yet to discover.'

'What else do you want from us?' Burdett asked.

Russell looked from Ben to his boss. 'You have given me what I wanted, which is another piece of the jigsaw. Now all I have to do is find out how it fits into the big picture. If there is anything, anything at all that comes to mind, call me. You have my number and if I'm not around you can always speak to Chris.' He motioned to Stamford, who nodded in agreement.

The two police officers left David Burdett's office leaving him slightly confused and Ben still in a state of shock. As they left, Burdett turned to Ben. 'You still look as if you've seen a ghost, Ben. How about you leave a bit early? You look as if you could with a lie down in a darkened room.'

Ben said that he would see how things went, but if it was ok he would like to finish after lunch. That was fine with Burdett who said to Ben that he hoped they wouldn't have to get involved in anything else.

Ben left the hotel at lunch-time, but before he left, he asked Sophie if she would go to his house that evening. She was always delighted at the thought of going to Ben's and said she would see him there at about six. When she had caught sight of him at the hotel she could see he was not himself and that he had lost all the colour from his cheeks.

That evening Ben, still a little shaken from the events of the day, met Sophie at his front door, and they made their way into the sitting room. Ben sat on the settee next to Sophie. He felt a wave of panic and again he started to shake.

'Ben, what's the matter?' Sophie cradled his head in her arms. She could feel him trembling.

'Sophie, something bad happened in Paris, something very bad.'

'What happened, Ben?' Sophie was really worried. 'Tell me, please.'

'I don't know if I can.' Sophie lifted his head so that she was looking directly into his eyes. 'Is it so bad that you can't tell me?'

'Sophie, it's tearing me apart and I don't know what to do.' She could see the struggle he was putting himself through. 'Tell me, Ben, please just tell me.'

Ben straightened himself and took hold of Sophie's hands. 'I'll tell you, Sophie, but you must promise not to breathe a word to a living soul about it, not even my aunt and uncle.'

'I promise, Ben, I really do.'

Ben then started to tell Sophie of his trip to Paris with Georges and how he thought he had been followed. He tried to tone down what took place in St Denis. Sophie gripped his hand harder as he told his story. When he had finished, Sophie was silent. They sat beside each other not knowing what to say. Their silence was broken when they heard a key being turned in the front door.

Ben looked at Sophie and whispered, 'Remember, not a word.' She nodded.

'What are you two up to?' Sarah entered the room.

'Just listening to some records.' Sophie tried to sound nonchalant.

'Are you staying tonight?'

Sophie jumped at the chance to stay with Ben, feeling he really needed her.

'Yes, please.'

'I hope you like sausages and mash because if you don't, you'll go hungry!'

'Umm, sounds great.' Sophie looked at Ben and squeezed his hand.

The next few days were full of torment for Ben. He kept visualising the photo of the dead man and remembering the feel of the tight band around his neck. It was not a pleasant time for him, but fortunately his shift pattern coincided with Sophie's and they decided to take some time away from everyone. Ben's friend Rodger had told Ben of a rather nice little pub that did accommodation near Amersham in Buckinghamshire, and you could get to it by train quite easily.

When Ben told Sophie that he thought it would do them good to get away, she agreed. She told Ben she would book two nights in the pub and that he was to leave everything to her. Sarah and Steven were pleased they would have some time alone.

'Perhaps things might develop, you never know,' Sarah said to Steven with a wink.

The weekend arrived more quickly than they had expected. Ben picked Sophie up at her flat and they made their way to Marylebone Station where they boarded the train. It wasn't a long journey, but being together away from the hotel and, although they hated to admit it, away from Ben's aunt and uncle, gave them a huge sense of relief. They sat and chatted about nothing in particular. The countryside rolled by and the watery sun shone in through the carriage window. They booked into the pub and hesitated when signing the register. The girl who booked them in just smiled at them and said they had young couples staying all the time, with or without wedding rings.

They had dinner in the pub, good honest grub which they enjoyed. After a drink in the bar, they made their way to their room. The night became one of nerves and apprehension. Should they, or shouldn't they? Their commitment to each other was total. They knew each other so well, yet felt strangely unsure of what to do. Embarrassment was something that had not bothered them since they first met, but being together in a double bed was a new experience. Sophie began to giggle at their nervousness and Ben joined in. They both laughed, then Ben took her in his arms and kissed her tenderly. 'You're the only person I want to spend my life with, Sophie.'

She pulled back slightly and looking directly into his eyes she whispered, 'I love you.'

They held each other close and became aware of each other's body. Ben slowly removed Sophie's top, his fingers shaking. Sophie felt a sudden surge of passion as they lay on the bed. Their clumsy attempts at safety made them both laugh, but nature took over and they found their way through pain to ecstasy. Sophie rested her head on Ben's chest and her eyes closed as they both fell into a deep sleep.

In the morning they went down to breakfast in the bar. A waitress asked what they would like, and without any hesitation Ben asked for a full English, and Sophie surprised him by saying that she would have one as well.

'After we've had our breakfast, I would like to get some fresh air. How about a nice walk in the countryside?'

The day was warming up as they left the pub. They noticed a sign for a bridal path and decided to take it. Ben looked up at the sign and then at the girl by his side, and his feelings for Sophie were so strong he knew he had to do something. Just how, or what, he wasn't quite sure. They had walked about half a mile when they came to a hill, and as they climbed it a vista of rolling countryside opened up before them. They stopped to feast on the view, and Ben put his arm round Sophie's waist and pulled her towards him.

'Sophie, will you marry me?'

Sophie was without words for once in her life. She had wondered if he might propose, but this was unexpected as they'd only come out for a walk. Her emotions were difficult to control. 'Oh *yes*, Ben.' She didn't say much, but that was all that was needed. They kissed, and their kiss was one of longing and love.

The following day was a Sunday and they spent the day trying to get their heads round the commitment they had just made to one another. Ben told Sophie that at the first opportunity they got he would whisk her off to the jeweller's and buy her a ring, the best he could afford.

Sophie laughed at him and said, 'It won't be a very expensive ring, then.'

That night they experienced each other in a different way, gentler and calmer than the previous night as they explored each other body, mind and soul.

Travelling back on the Monday they discussed how they would tell Sophie's dad and Ben's aunt and uncle. Sophie wanted Ben to come to her flat that evening when they would tell her dad, and if they could tell Ben's aunt and uncle the following day together, that would be great. 'But can you keep a secret from Sarah and Steven until I arrive? she asked Ben teasingly.

'I will do my best!'

Their plan worked out well. Sophie's dad was not surprised by their announcement and told them they had left it long enough. They decided that, as soon as Ben's aunt and uncle had been told, they would celebrate. Ben knew that his aunt would demand they hold some sort of party at their house and he could see her making arrangements already.

They met after the last serving had been successfully delivered and made their way to Ben's house. When they arrived, Sarah and Steven were watching television. They walked into the sitting room, where Ben took his aunt and uncle by surprise saying that he would like to introduce them to his fiancé. It took a few moments for the message to sink in, then Sarah jumped up and threw her arms round Sophie saying that it was a wonderful moment and welcome to the family. Steven stood and shook Ben's hand.

'Well done, lad. I thought it might have been sooner but you got there in the end.'

Sarah was immediately into one of her 'got to do something' states: Steven we must have a party, yes a party, and you young lady will be by my side, so who will we invite, when shall we arrange it, what shall we do about ... so much to think of ...

Steven suggested his wife calm down and that there was plenty of time to organise things.

Two weeks after his proposal, the party took place. Ben's house was full. There were those from the hotel, others from Steven's company, lots of Sarah's friends, some Ben had never seen let alone met. College friends came when they heard the word 'party'; altogether it was a great bunch of people. The drink flowed and a mountain of food was consumed. Ben looked across the room at Sophie and blew her a kiss. Although he was on top of the world, he had to stop and take stock when Annabel Stewart and Peter Russell joined the party. Sophie told Ben that she had to invite Annabel because she had done so much for her, and Ben agreed that of course she should.

When Peter Russell spoke to Ben, however, he felt a shiver run down his back and his face went white.

'I've just spoken to your boss, Ben, to let him know that the case you were involved with has been taken as far as it can. Which is thanks to you both identifying the photograph. We have managed to piece together some recent activity here and in Paris and found that Max Steyning was part of an organisation that had been dealing in drugs for quite some time. In fact, Steyning had been responsible for the supply of various classes of drugs through a network of clubs he had been running since the early sixties. I guess he was responsible for quite a few youngsters losing their way.'

Peter wished Ben all the luck in the world and told him he was a very lucky guy to have captured someone like Sophie. Sophie saw him talking to Ben and she noticed the immediate change in him. He seemed to stiffen as Peter approached and he looked very pale. She walked over and apologised to Peter and Annabel, saying she had to steal him away to meet other guests.

Ben's uncle appeared and started to talk to Peter and Annabel about decimalisation, which Sophie knew would either keep them entranced or make them head for the hills.

She gripped Ben's arm. 'Are you ok?'

'Yes, I'm fine. I just had a flashback, but I'm alright now. I just wish my brother could have been here.' *I'm sorry I couldn't have done more, Jack, but I guess I've played a part.* 'Perhaps he can sleep easy now.'

*

In one of the more exclusive residential areas of Rome, the Villa Sienna stands back from the edge of the Via Di Valle Delle Camene, its neo-classical frontage denoting wealth and power. Its interior was lavishly furnished. In the main dining room, eight men sat around a large mahogany table, having just finished a rather excellent meal. The dishes were removed by a tall military-type figure who efficiently cleared the table after each course. He finally disappeared from the room, only to return moments later with eight leather folders which he placed in front of each of the eight diners. He then placed three glass jugs of iced lemon water in the centre of the table.

The person at the head of the table started to speak, his face giving little away and his accent the low monotone of Birmingham. All eyes turned in his direction.

'Gentlemen, my name is Joseph. I have spoken briefly to you all on the telephone, but due to operational difficulties experienced in London and Paris, I would like to confirm a change in the management structure, which has expanded somewhat from our previous meeting in London. I have been placed in charge of the European sector. For your information, Max, as you will know from newspaper reports, is no longer available, and Adam has regrettably decided to take early retirement.'

Those around the table looked at each other, knowing exactly what 'early retirement' involved.

'If you open your folders, you will find a full agenda for this evening's meeting. We have a great deal to discuss so I suggest we make a start …'

Printed by: Copytech (UK) Limited trading as
Printondemand-worldwide.com
9 Culley Court, Bakewell Road, Orton Southgate,
Peterborough, PE2 6XD